# Lauriat

# Lauriat

A FILIPINO-CHINESE
SPECULATIVE FICTION ANTHOLOGY

## Edited by Charles Tan

LETHE PRESS • MAPLE SHADE, NJ

Published in 2012 by Lethe Press, Inc.
118 Heritage Avenue • Maple Shade, NJ 08052-3018
www.lethepressbooks.com • lethepress@aol.com
ISBN: 1-59021-254-1
ISBN-13: 978-1-59021-254-7

These stories are works of fiction. Names, characters, places, and incidents are products of the authors' imaginations or are used fictitiously.

Set in Warnock, Myriad, and Palatino.
Interior design: Alex Jeffers.
Cover artwork and design: Maxie Wei.

LIBRARY OF CONGRESS CATALOGING-IN-PUBLICATION DATA
  Lauriat : a Filipino-Chinese speculative fiction anthology / edited by Charles Tan.
    p. cm.
  ISBN-13: 978-1-59021-254-7 (pbk. : alk. paper)
  ISBN-10: 1-59021-254-1 (pbk. : alk. paper)
  1. Speculative fiction, Philippine (English) 2. Science fiction, Philippine (English) 3. Chinese--Philippines. I. Tan, Charles.
  PR9550.8.L38 2012
  820.8'09599--dc23
                    2012014699

# Table of Contents

*Dedicated to the editors who have inspired me:*
*Ellen Datlow, Terri Windling, Jonathan Strahan, Rich*
*Horton, John Joseph Adams, Gavin Grant and Kelly Link,*
*Steve Berman.*

# Introduction

## Charles Tan

I IDENTIFY MYSELF as Filipino-Chinese, and while that demographic is represented in Philippine literature from established writers like Caroline Hau, Charlson Ong, Ricky Lee, or the late Doreen Yu, it's sorely lacking when it comes to the speculative fiction genre. Not that there's a shortage of local Filipino-Chinese SF writers—as will hopefully be proven by this anthology—but rather the Filipino-Chinese condition is seldom discussed in our SF stories. I didn't even consider writing a Filipino-Chinese character in my fiction until I was approached by Derwin Mak and Eric Choi to contribute to their Chinese-themed anthology, *The Dragon and the Stars*, three years ago. For the past few years, I've been promoting Philippine SF, but it only recently occurred to me to become more hands-on when it comes to Filipino-Chinese literature. No one yet has assembled an anthology on Filipino-Chinese SF, and Lethe Press thankfully gave me that opportunity.

If you're reading this, looking to discover a broad, sweeping generalization about what Filipino-Chinese SF is like, then my answer will disappoint you: I don't know. Instead, I wanted to see what our writers would come up with, given my two constraints: 1) come up with a SF story and 2) it has to have a Filipino-Chinese element to it. While some stories headed in the direction I expected, others surprised me and caught me off guard. It was also interesting to discover how a lot of the submitted stories contained an element of horror.

Perhaps another tricky subject when talking about Filipino-Chinese SF is who I considered to be Filipino-Chinese. Heritage is always a tricky subject—my family being a good example of Chinese purity and prejudice: whenever I'd bring a friend to the house, the first thing my parents would ask was whether they were Chinese or Filipino, and would speak about the latter with contempt. A lot of Filipino-Chinese families I know even forbid their children from marrying someone that wasn't of "pure" Chinese blood (i.e. someone whose parents are both Chinese), even if they themselves had broken that taboo by marrying a Filipino. What's interesting about the Filipino-Chinese experience is that it's diverse and encapsulates many different combinations. For my contributors, I attempted to solicit from a diverse group, some of which only loosely identify themselves as Filipino-Chinese. Hopefully the stories in this anthology encapsulate that diversity.

Last but not least is the title of this book: *Lauriat*. What exactly is a Lauriat? It's a eight-, nine-, ten-course dinner featuring a variety of dishes, everything from noodles to abalone to Peking duck to lobster. It's an apt description for this not-quite-themed anthology, and is a popular Filipino-Chinese tradition.

I'm not fond of introductions that attempt to explain the stories so I'll end here. I hope you enjoy reading this book.

ANDREW DRILON *has been telling stories through the medium of comics for almost a decade now. He first ventured into the realm of prose fiction in order to improve his abilities as a comics writer, and quickly found himself enamored by the form. Since then, his short stories have been published in* The Philippines Free Press, Bewildering Stories, The Philippine Daily Inquirer, Ladlad 3, The Virtuous Medlar Circle, Philippine Genre Stories, The Apex Book of World SF, *volume 2, and* Chalomot Be'aspamia *(an Israeli specfic magazine). He was a finalist for the Philippines Free Press Literary Awards and a recipient of The Philippine Graphic/Fiction Award.*

# Two Women Worth Watching

## Andrew Drilon

DARIEL IS LUCKY to have gotten so close. Lourdes too, in this crowd. Huan is above them, getting a better view. Jonabet has been waiting all year. Xiangzu is excited. Simeon is amused. Genevieve is wondering what it's all about. Basti considers the familiar waiter then focuses back on the scene.

Mia and Faye are having dinner at Café Bonita. It's more of an upscale restaurant than a café. It has a *Newsweek* article framed on the wall by the doorway. They serve fusion Filipino cuisine—*kare-kare* stew with melted swiss cheese, focaccia bread and *bangus* pâté, fresh corned beef dipped in hoisin sauce; standards mashed-up with strangeness. The food is so good that you have to place a reservation weeks in advance in order to get a table. The wait list is filled with names of the rich and famous.

Faye's assistant handled all the details, securing a table for two in a private VIP room. All Mia had to do was show up. They do this twice a year, because Faye likes to know that she still has some friends in the world. Mia has been her closest confidante since they were both fifteen. They were best friends in high school, and tonight they're pretending they still are.

"Try the two-way *adobo*," Mia says. "So good. It's crispy and soft at the same time."

"I don't know," says Faye. "I shouldn't eat so much. I'm near my weight limit."

"Oh, right. Maybe not. What about the *ming-ming laing*? It's all vegetables, right?"

"Yes it is. Okay. Also the Bikol Express?"

"Doesn't that have milk?"

"So does the *laing*."

"Faye! We have to eat something."

Their little room is overflowing with people. The door opens and a waiter comes over. He recognizes Faye immediately. He's seen her on TV. The other girl is not so familiar, but has a certain quality about her. She speaks in a loud, high pitch. Her movements are exaggerated and dramatic. Theatrical. The waiter is convinced that these are important people, and takes extra care to comport himself with dignity. He might get a big tip out of this.

"Your orders, ma'am?"

"One garlic *ma-chang*, one Bikol Express, one *ming-ming laing* and two Vietnamese iced coffees," Mia says. "Is it really from Vietnam?"

"Yes, ma'am. Ca Phe Hoa Tan. It's flown in every Thursday."

"You know," says Faye, "I had a shoot in Vietnam last year. It was depressing. But the coffee was good."

Mia smiles. The waiter walks off with their orders. He brushes past his great-grandfather, Basti, who died in the Japanese invasion of Bataan. They ignore each other. Basti stands next to Mia, who sits across from Faye. You could say he was attracted by the crowd. He views this rare biannual event with much curiosity.

Faye is visiting from Los Angeles, where she works for most of the year. She is an international silver-screen celebrity. Her résumé is full of commercials, endorsements, primetime television awards and summer blockbuster roles. Mia is a celebrity too, but Faye doesn't know it, because she does not perceive the dead. Faye has her share of perceptions, but she cannot account for all of them. She has seen and done so much in her lifetime. All her relationships are complicated and uncertain, filled with subtexts she can barely grasp.

If Faye were more articulate, she might have been able to explain how she has made an impressive living off of perception; how her life has been dedicated to making others see what they want to see. "It's an industry of prettified lies, where the surface is all that matters," she might have said. But she didn't, because Faye is not very articulate. All her best lines are written for her. Anyway, she'd have been wrong, because Hollywood is filled with dead people, and the dead can see the truth. Death makes sense that way.

Mia is a sensible woman. She has a huge fan base among the dead. It dwarfs Faye's by a significant margin. There are so many more dead people than living, after all. Every night, before going to sleep, Mia makes sure to say her daily coda: "You make me every day," and, after a measured pause: "This one's for you." It's a snappy shout-out that builds familiarity, comforting the audience and, above all, acknowledging them. Mia might be the only living person who does this on a regular basis. It's a time-tested formula that's worked for her since she was fifteen.

Mia, like you, cannot see the dead, but she has decided that they are watching. Lourdes remembers when this lifelong decision began. Mia was six years old when her grandmother first told her about the dead. In the Philippines, almost everyone's grandmother can see the dead, and Mia's was no exception. Some say it's a racial ability, or perhaps linked to archipelagic geography. The Seven Thousand Islands have long been a popular afterlife hotspot. Bakana passed away in Groote Eylandt; Wency in Ouachita; Norton in Northampton; Leehom in Lào Cai. Like many others, they moved here to settle down. There is a healthier respect for the dead here, and it's not as depressing as Vietnam.

"I read this article in the *Times*," says Faye, making conversation. "It's about how everyone is obsessed with fame these days. They say attention is the global currency of the twenty-first century."

Mia smiles. "I think it's been the currency a lot longer than that."

"Speaking of which, I heard you came into a lot of money last month. Another lotto win?"

"Actually, it was an investment paying off. That was a big moment for me, taking that out. I placed it when I was twenty-one."

"Wow. You're the luckiest person I know, Mia. Someone's watching over you."

"Please. It's nothing. You probably make ten times as much in a year."

"Maybe. But I need to work so hard for it. All you have to do is sign papers and you're good."

"That's not true. I work hard, too. I have a busy schedule."

"Charity races? Extreme sports? Singing contests? That's not work, Mia. That's fun."

Zondria disagrees, as do a few others. There are 59,483 people in Café Bonita tonight. One hundred forty-seven of them are alive, checking their mobiles, mistiming jokes, eating and breathing through awkward pauses, all thinking about things they'd rather not think. The hairs rise on their arms and they assume it's the air conditioning. The rest are invisible. Many stand in empty spaces. Their feet do not touch the ground. Some are pressed halfway through walls while others suspend themselves from the ceiling. A few of them—children—are hanging from the chandeliers. Everyone is intent on Mia and Faye's table.

Mia takes a breath. She wants to say how difficult her life has been from moment to moment, but doesn't want to come off as whiny. She wants to talk about the delicate balance she needs to maintain, but doesn't want to seem boastful. Bragging does no good if you're in a story; it only eradicates sympathy and sets you up for a fall. She decides on the humble route. It's not like she needs Faye's approval. Faye is a supporting character; a guest star at best. She isn't Mia's audience.

"I do stuff," Mia says then shakes her head. "No, you're right. Your work is probably harder than mine. But it's worth it, right? Everyone's so proud of you. You're going places. And your last co-star was gorgeous."

Faye smiles. He was a gorgeous *gweilo*; that last one. He said she was beautiful. Faye likes compliments. She was a lanky, long-chinned girl when she was young, and didn't get much attention until she was older. Her mother says she grew into her face. Her mother says a lot of things. Talk to that producer. Get a better stylist. You can't go over your weight limit. Faye's mother has a way with words. She says that Faye isn't especially good-looking, but the oddness of her features makes her memorable. Faye got her chin from her father. That *lun tao*. Never did anything to make her happy.

Happiness: that about sums it up, doesn't it? We all want to be happy. Faye wants to be happy. The waiter wants to be happy. Niccolo, Qiang, Mechu, you. It's the core, abstract goal that we all strive toward. Even the dead want it. The question is how to get it. Dominic recalls Mia asking the question twenty years ago:

"*Ama*, how can I be happy?"

That was at her grandmother's house, a dilapidated two-storey villa weathered down by four generations of family. It was Ghost Month, and they had been lighting long sticks of *xiāng* at the family *shén tán* when Mia brought up the broad idea of happiness. Her grandmother had scoffed, steadied herself on the altar, looked up at the statue of their ancestor and replied:

"Ah, *baobei*. That is a difficult question to answer. As we grow into the world, we must each decide what will make us happy. It is different for each person. For some, it is money. For others, it is love. For you, it might be recognition, success or achievement. Most people must settle for the happiness they are given."

"What if I get all those things at once, *ama*? Then I'll be happy for sure!"

"Perhaps," her grandmother had said. She was nearing death at that point, Mia's *ama*. Her body was wracked with arthritis, rheumatism, Parkinson's, osteoporosis and more. The maids said she was crazy with pain, and perhaps too far gone to even think properly. Perhaps she was thinking straight for the first time in her life. There is a singular clarity that comes with being so close to death's door. Mia's grandmother knew she wouldn't be able to communicate once the threshold was crossed, and she was carrying more than a few jewels of knowledge with her. She must have thought it was a good time to share.

"There is a way, my little *baobei*. Happiness is fickle and fleeting, but if you enjoy many blessings and look forward to many more, you can be happy all your life. But to attain that—well, you must first understand the nature of the dead."

Mia had listened and understood. Six years old is the perfect age to be told such things. Most of us tend to grow out of our sense of the dead as we approach our teens, but Mia was still young enough to keep hold of it. Her grandmother spoke of how people still exist after their bodies perish; of their circuitous habits and voyeuristic tendencies and much,

much more. The dead crowd the streets of the world, bored and aimless, looking for things of interest. Since they cannot partake of food or indulge their sexual appetites, they take pleasure from watching the living.

"Some prove to be more popular than others," her grandmother had said. "And you, *baobei*, have all the potential to be a star. You have so much ahead of you; so many ways to do it right. They say that where the dead go, blessings follow. The dead have no use for such things, so they pass it on to those who amuse them most. Beauty, luck, good health, prosperity—all these things are yours for the taking if you can but entertain such an audience."

"How can I do that, *ama*?"

"Your life must become a performance."

There had been thirty-nine people observing them at the time, thirty of whom are now crowding around Mia and Faye, watching their every move. The nine others have gone on to become self-appointed marketers, spreading word of Mia's performance among their fellow dead. It's important to build an audience that can sustain itself, even through lay or mundane periods. Excitement begets excitement. Boring can be build-up. Tedium becomes anticipation.

Mia has learned that an interesting life tends to perpetuate itself. A secret kiss, an unpaid debt, a stolen glance, a goal announced—she doesn't have to do much in order to set the wheels in motion. It's the maintenance that gets taxing. Side-plots evolve into full-fledged story arcs; themes demand satisfaction; minor characters blossom into dark reflections.

"They can say what they want," says Faye. "I don't care."

"But doesn't it get to you?" Mia says. "The tweets, the hate blogs, the message boards—you get so much bad press."

"People don't hate me. They can't. They don't even know me. If they hated me, they wouldn't watch. That's just confusing me with my character. And the tabloids."

"I wouldn't know what to do if people hated me."

"No one hates you, Mia. You're very likeable."

In the past two decades, Mia has become quite adept at her performance. There is a method and manner to how she lives. She brushes her hair every day and maintains excellent hygiene. She manages a large cast of supporting characters—family, friends, lovers, acquaintances, enemies. She pursues challenges at every opportunity. Whether she succeeds or not doesn't matter, so long as there is a sense of difficulty. Like you, the dead enjoy watching conflict. *Schadenfreude* thrills them, as do music and spectacle and loss. With the right mix, you can get a whole lot of them to watch you all the time.

Faye has her own method of performing. Internalize the character. Embrace the situation. Surrender to the emotion. She has a way of squinting and crinkling her nose; a visual tic that she inserts into every performance, like a signature. She's more comfortable as other characters. It's when she's herself that she's bothered. Faye suspects that her soul is growing smaller and smaller. She had a nightmare, once, of a camera-shaped proboscis drawing away her *qi*; her life force; her very essence. Faye's therapist chalked it up to depression and gave her a bottle of Citalopram. She's felt blurry and detached ever since. Almost everyone talks to her with an air of pretension. Mia isn't one of them. Mia understands her. They'll always be best friends.

"The waiter's been staring at me since we got here. It's creepy."

"Shouldn't you be used to that by now?"

"No. Not really. That's why I never went Broadway. I can't stand to see too many eyeballs. I'm fine with a crew and cameras. You don't have to see everyone watching."

"I guess that would make it easier."

The waiter has come to the conclusion that he needs a picture of himself with Faye. He plans to take it with his phone and post it online. His friends in Bataan will be green with envy. They'll think he's made something of himself. Maybe someone will interview him in the newspaper or put him on TV. Wouldn't that be amazing? It's against Café Bonita policy to harass customers, but he figures he can swing it later, while she waits for the valet. He'll punch out, take off his uniform, put on his favorite Makabayan shirt and ask her for a picture. It has to look casual, though. It has to look like they're friends. The loud girl can join in too, if she wants.

Mia is quite content with where she is right now. At ten years old, she had a total of fifty followers. The number grew as she got older, in ones and twos each year. She lucked out in high school, when she dated a third-generation legacy celebrity and managed to hijack his 1,562 viewers. They had been trailing him out of loyalty to his grandfather, and were growing bored anyway. Mia attended a concert in Araneta Coliseum and nabbed another couple thousand by getting arrested in front of a camera. She took a dance class in Malate, enchanted a hot gay *barkada* and picked up over three thousand deceased homosexuals. There weren't that many dead in Singapore, but she grabbed a boatload of them on her way back from Hong Kong. The dead can see each other, after all, and with the numbers Mia was pulling, her crowd was enough to attract more. Her *ama* had mentioned that at higher levels, popularity achieves a kind of snowball effect. Mia is now pushing 60k.

"Mia, you remember Dariel? That *mestizo* guy you dated in high school? I got an invite to his funeral last year, but couldn't make it. Did you go?"

"Oh my god, Faye. I didn't know. What happened?"

"Overdose, I think. I'm not clear on the details. They found him in a parking lot."

"Poor Dariel." Mia sighs. "He was such a nice guy."

Dariel beams from the far wall. His fellow viewers acknowledge his relevance before turning back to Mia. Dariel only ever slept with Mia in order to get close to Faye, but now he realizes what he once had. Mia has clearly put a lot of thought into this. She's never said it out loud, but she suspects that the amount of dead viewers is directly proportional to how much living a person does over a year. Not every day has to be exciting. Many attention-crazed people go wild in their youth and burn out early. The urgency of the living demands constant entertainment, but the dead have longer attention spans. Mia has pegged it at around five weeks, a sizeable period of engagement before interest begins to wane. Running plotlines like her disillusionment with her father and her search for true love serve to keep longtime viewers hooked. Romantic issues are always a crowd-pleaser.

For the benefit of new followers, she tries to build up to an event at least once a month. Mountain climbing, rave parties, intense breakups, family spats—the specifics don't really matter so long as the event is contrived and exciting. Her next one is sex with a half-paralyzed fashion photographer. She's been building up to it for weeks. This dinner with Faye is just a holding action; a prelude.

"Have you thought about settling down?" asks Faye.

"Haven't found the right one yet. That's me: bachelorette for life." Mia lets out a controlled sigh, for effect.

"I was thinking about becoming a producer. I haven't told my agent yet. I've been so busy and it might knock me out for a year. I'm not sure we can handle it."

"You can do it. I believe in you, Faye. You always have good ideas."

"Speak for yourself. Seriously, maybe we should team up. It's not like you need credentials."

"Seriously? I'd love to, but I couldn't. I've got too much going on here."

Mia is finished after two spoonfuls of *laing*. Her glass of Vietnamese coffee is half-empty. Faye has polished off her plate, the Bikol Express and the bowl of garlic *ma-chang*. The waiter returns.

"How about dessert, ma'am? We have *biko à la mode* and lychee panna cotta."

"Mia?"

"No thank you. I think we're good."

Faye smiles at the waiter; squints and crinkles her nose. Mia makes an offer but Faye refuses. "It's on me," she says. Mia likes to get involved in other people's business on occasion; a sure bet for extra drama. But Faye is off-limits; to be kept at arm's length; forever relegated to guest star status. She fears that Faye steals some of her audience every time they meet. It's a cute, groundless fear that makes her all the more riveting. Mia can feel too real—too mundane—around Faye. It's like talking to your grandmother.

The waiter rushes off to the kitchen, hands in the bill, punches out, switches to casual clothes and runs out the back door. He doubles-back through a side-street, running toward the front entrance to meet Faye. A car veers around the corner, too fast for him to avoid. There is shrapnel in the air and shrieks of alarm, but he is already displaced, watching from beyond the threshold. He sees the women walk out of Café Bonita, poised and elegant. They stop at the commotion, but decide to leave anyway. They kiss each other and promise to meet again. The waiter sees Faye get into her car. No one is following her, but droves of dead people are trailing after Mia. He sees his great-grandfather, Basti, walking among them. They speak briefly and decide to attend a show together.

Back at her hotel, Faye slips out of high heels and makes her way to the bedroom. She sits on the bed and turns on the television. She flips through channels and happens upon a late-night showing of *The Golden Lake*. It was her first movie. She watches herself striding through glittering palaces, fan in hand, hungry for attention. The handsome *jiedushi* presents her to the imperial court. She is a commodity; a coin spent for political gain. The courtiers fawn and applaud her obedience as she is given over to the emperor.

Faye looks so radiant onscreen, she thinks, back when she still had a soul. She remembers her mother and the camera and her dream of being a producer, all somehow so distant. She goes to the bathroom, drinks down a tab of Citalopram and takes a good long look at her reflection. No one is watching. The dead are absent from her hotel suite. Something about her repels them. She is too obvious; too clichéd. Let the living enjoy her. Faye has been alone since Mia left.

Two miles and three kilometers away, the dead have congregated around a beautifully-restored two-storey villa. Some hang from the roof, suspended. Some loiter in the streets, unable to get in. The inside is packed with spectators, standing shoulder-to-shoulder, crawling up the walls, their presence getting thicker and thicker toward the bedroom, where the most dedicated viewers wait, having maintained their priority seats over the span of years. All eyes and ears and senses are trained on a single living person, humming a tune in the shower. Mia dries her hair and steps out of the bathroom. She is completely naked. Her bedroom only seems empty. Every inch of space around her, the world and all it contains, is her stage. She gives a knowing wink at nothingness before turning out the lights. It's time to treat her audience to something special. One day, she hopes, someone will do the same for her.

A steady beat in her chest. A tap on the wall. Mia strides to the center of the room and takes her position at the foot of the bed. Lungs expand and contract as she performs a dance in the dark; a sweet, improvised contemporary piece accompanied only by the thrum of the air conditioner and the rush of cars passing outside. Her body flails, arms outstretched, legs arched then falling to the rhythm of her heartbeat, which rises to the occasion. It crescendos, they cheer, she gasps and as the dance winds down to an end, her feet are almost hesitant to touch the ground. Shadows roister around her. Mia's grandmother is among them, proud as can be. Mia can feel it, deep down inside. She's not so real anymore. She's moving in and out of people, touching them as she goes. It's exhilarating.

"You made me. All of you. You make me every day." She spins and gestures. "This one's for you."

There is an echo of applause. Mia grins and takes a bow. She falls into her bed, sinking into the sheets, spent but fulfilled. The dead watch on, transfixed. In the stillness, as her breath begins to calm, she imagines the years ahead; overflowing with blessings. She is so happy she could die. And eventually, like everyone else, she does.

ERIN CHUPECO's *been a tech writer, a digital artist, an IT specialist for a presidential campaign, an events planner and marketing executive, an activist, a freelance travel and gaming writer and, most recently, a wife. Now maintains a writing blog (http://www.paperheroes. net), a small business, and a sense of humor. Currently working on a novel.*

# Ho-We

## Erin Chupeco

THERE IS A nose staring up at me across the dining room table; lying on top of a piece of napkin, right beside mother's fine China plate. Mother told me later that it was a *decomposing* nose, and *Achi* said it smelled of raw sewage and *mediocrity*. I looked up 'decompose' in the dictionary, and it meant to "separate or break down into constituent parts." I also looked up 'mediocrity', which meant "of only ordinary or moderate quality." I like looking things up in the dictionary, and my teachers say I have excellent vocabulary ("words used by a particular group of people for communication") for my age. I agree with mother, but I don't think I agree with *Achi*, because it was the least ordinary nose that I had ever seen.

There was a nose on the table mostly, I think, because of father. Father's name is Tony Lauzon, and he is the chairman and CEO of a company called United Holdings, Inc. He is also the president of the homeowner's association of the Gated Hills subdivision, which is what the neighborhood we live in is called. Father disapproves of a lot of things. He disapproves of lazy people. He disapproves of the number four. He disapproves of big Filipino families, because they always throw big *fiestas* in the provinces and ask him to help pay afterwards, and because they are leeches. Leeches are "any worm of the class Hirudinea, often used for bloodletting." I saw leeches on the Discovery Channel on cable once, and they don't look like Filipino families to me. Maybe father meant "people who cling to another in order to achieve personal gain," which is another definition for leeches. It was father who insisted that *Achi* bring Gary over for dinner, and it was making *Achi* uncomfortable.

"The nose is staring at me," *Achi* whispered. *Achi* is actually Marcella Amanda Lauzon, my oldest sister. She is thirty years old, but she is not yet married. *Achi* and I look a little like father, with our large eyes and bumpy noses and big ears. *Di-chi* and *Sa-chi* both resemble my mother, who has a pointed chin and soft slanted eyes and a pretty complexion ("a natural color, texture and appearance of a person's skin, often his or her face"). *Di-chi*'s name is Abigail, and she is twenty eight and married to a minotaur from mainland China who owns a big textile ("cloth or material produced by weaving, knitting, or sewing") business. *Sa-chi*'s name is Leilani, and she is twenty three and had just recently married a Taiwanese half-dragon who owns a bottling company. I am not married, but that's because father said I can only have a *ho-we* when I'm in college, and that's still a million years away. *Ho-we* means "boyfriend" or "lover" in Hokkien Chinese, which is one of three languages that father speaks.

Sometimes I imagine that when I am old enough I would get a *ho-we* who is part gargoyle, so he can fly me over the traffic in Manila instead of having to go through it. Or a merman, so we can live under the sea and have a pet whale. *Achi* laughs when I tell her this. "It would be hard for you to have children if you marry a merman," she said. I don't know what she meant, but she said she would tell me when I was older. *Achi* is a UP scholar and studied economics in college. Whenever father is angry he sometimes asks what is the point of being smart if it didn't help *Achi* find a husband anyway.

It probably seems strange to everyone else that *Di-chi* and *Sa-chi* married first before *Achi* had. I know father thinks so.

I was sitting beside *Achi* now, pretending to cut up the fried pork chop on my plate and trying hard not to stare at the nose myself, and I heard what she had said. I thought that was strange, because noses don't have eyes. "Don't be silly dear," mother murmured back, "and don't be rude to our guest."

Our guest was a boy named Gary Cheng, and he met *Achi* through a *kai-shao* arranged by father and Gary's father. "*Kai-shao*" wasn't listed in the dictionary, but mother explained that it was like a blind date. I thought that meant Gary was blind, but mother said it meant that the people going on the date had never met each other before, because it was arranged by mutual friends or family instead. I thought it all sounded very complicated.

I bet if *Achi* knew her date had a decomposing nose she would have never agreed to the *kai-shao*.

*Achi* didn't like Gary. She went on two dates with him and said she didn't want to go out with him anymore, but father began treating Gary like he was really *Achi*'s boyfriend. "How's Gary doing?" my father would ask, or "Why don't you call up Gary and invite him to watch a movie with you?" or "We're going on a family trip this November, maybe Gary would like to come along." Anyone would have thought that Gary was father's boyfriend and not *Achi*'s, and Gary wasn't even *Achi*'s real boyfriend.

Father normally hates messiness, but he didn't say anything about Gary's nose. He even sounded happy about it. "You have to be careful about what you young people eat," he said. "So much fatty food and oils they serve at restaurants nowadays. You'll be getting a heart attack before you even reach my age."

"Gary's heart stopped three years ago," *Achi* said, but father ignored her. "Good healthy food and lots of exercise," father said, with conviction ("in a state of firm belief"). "That'll keep the nose on your face for at least twenty more years."

I wondered if they had healthy food for zombies, like vegetarian entrails ("the internal organs of animals") or soya blood. But I read in the news the other day about this guy who married a dog to get rid of a curse someone had put on him, and a guy who ate his underwear so he could pass a drunk driving test. So maybe anything is possible.

Mother said it's a running joke in the family that father would never like a boy that *Achi* likes, and *Achi* would never like a boy that father likes, except I don't understand how a joke could run and neither father nor Marcie thought it was funny.

"Sorry," Gary said. Or at least, that's what I thought he said. Actually, what I heard was "Suhr-rauugh-yyy."

"A polite boy," father said as an aside to mother, beaming. *Achi* folded her arms over her chest, not looking happy.

Inviting *Achi*'s boyfriends over to dinner was never father's idea, it was always mother's. She wanted him to see the boyfriend first before deciding if he liked him. Father was angry whenever this happened, but he usually agreed in the end. Mother is always calm when she argues with father about *Achi*'s boyfriends. She says it's because she knows she's right.

"You need to get to know them better first before you start forbidding her to go out with them, Tony," she said reassuringly. "You're not being fair to Marcie."

"I don't need to know them better to know that they aren't good enough, Ann," father said.

*Achi* had four boyfriends before agreeing to the *kai-shao*. Their names were Eric, Peter, Howie-J, and Gilgamesh. Father never liked any of them.

Mother always thought well of *Achi's* ex-boyfriends, though. She liked Eric's smooth pale complexion and well-kept fangs, and thought him kindhearted. Peter always looked dashing and took great care with how he looks, and he was always so polite. Howard was always careful not to break things and overturn the furniture whenever he visited. Like the time he accidentally knocked over her Swarovski crystal cabinet but caught every figurine before they smashed against the floor. She liked his voice, the way he always asked after her and brought her flowers on Mother's Day. Howard, I think, was mother's favorite of *Achi's* boyfriends.

Eric's full name was Eric Theodore Gonzales, and he was a one-hundred-and-thirty-four-year old vampire who died during the Philippine Revolution ("a period of change, often through drastic means") of 1896. He was a member of the Katipuneros who were fighting under Andres Bonifacio's banner, and he was killed when a Spaniard stabbed him from behind with a bayonet ("a sharp, pointed weapon attached to the muzzle of a firearm").He even showed me the scar that the bayonet left, which was a long ugly-looking puckered line running down his lower back. It was the coolest thing I had ever seen, but father wasn't impressed. Two days before the dinner, he promised *Achi* a brand new Ford Explorer if she would break up with Eric. She said no, and then she said other words mother wouldn't want me saying because I'm not old enough.

"Aren't you a little too old to be dating my daughter?" Father had snapped the first time *Achi* had brought Eric over for dinner, glaring at the vampire over his glasses.

"I was nineteen when I died, sir," Eric said politely.

"And I don't see how his age's got to do with anything," Marcie said hotly.

"It's got everything to do with it," Father said. "I'm not going to have people gossip about you going about with a man six times your age, especially a *hwana* who used to go around shooting people." He squinted back at Eric. "How many people have you bitten?" He demanded. "If you've bitten my daughter, I'm calling the mayor, he's a friend of mine."

"He was a Katipunero!" Marcie snapped back angrily. "A hero! Stop treating him like a criminal!"

"Not good enough," Father said.

While father and Marcie retired into the den to argue, Eric quietly showed me how he could bend a fork nearly in half, and then straighten it out again. He was very strong. His skin was milky white, though he said he was very dark back when he was alive, and his eyes were yellowing around the corners, but he had a nice smile.

"You're thirty-nine, aren't you Gary?" Father was asking now. "About to turn forty this September? Forty years young!" He chuckled. Gary's father is one of father's business colleagues ("a person whom one works with, especially in business") and a close friend, so father probably knew more about Gary than *Achi* did. "I hear you're planning a big birthday celebration—Marcie's invited, of course? That's what George said." George was Gary's father.

Gary made an odd gurgling sound. Then he picked his nose up with crumbly fingers and tried to stick it back into the hole in his face. I quickly looked away, but then I looked back again, because that's what people say about a car wreck—you can't look away even when you want to. I was expecting more of Gary to fall off, like an ear or an arm or a leg. *Achi* glared down at her food in disgust.

After Eric and *Achi* broke up, she began dating Peter Battacharjee, an Indian werewolf. He was so tall that his head nearly reached the ceiling of our house, but he was always very clean and his clothes were the latest men's fashions. I thought all werewolves had dark beards and were hairy, but Peter was bald and very clean-shaven, and he had a pierced left ear, like a musician.

Father didn't care that Peter was tall or had a nicely shaped head or had good clothes. He started grilling him about his eating habits and his nocturnal ("usually attributed to an animal or species active during night time") lifestyle, and if he knew anything about the stabbing incident that happened during the last full moon over at Shaw Boulevard. Father and *Achi* almost immediately got into a fight after Peter left.

"I'm not going to let any daughter of mine date some *bombay* who sleeps all day because he likes to sneak around at night attacking people!" Father snapped. "Have you seen those teeth? Why else would he be always awake at night?"

"Because he works the nightshift at Accenture!" *Achi* shrieked. "He's senior team leader!"

"Not good enough," Father announced.

Father and *Achi* stopped talking to each other for months after that incident, and only started again after *Achi* had broken up with Peter.

"Gary manages a big American account," Father told mother and me. "George says he's been trained in the States and in London. Hardworking, just like his dad—I wouldn't have gone into business with him if he wasn't!"

Father laughed like it was another joke. I smiled wanly ("weak, lacking in vitality"), because I didn't really know what to say, and then mother said something else, but I wasn't really listening. *Achi* was scowling.

*Achi*'s next boyfriend was Howie-J, a deejay who worked for Smash Station 103.9. I've heard his voice many times over the radio, and he talked in a rough, husky baritone ("a male voice lighter in range than a bass but lower than a tenor") which is why he has lots of female fans. His real name is Howard Joachim Abellardo, but he says he's gotten so used to being called Howie-J that sometimes he forgets to respond when people call him Howard.

I remember the first time Howie-J came over for dinner. I was running down the stairs without looking where I was going, and crashed into a large hairy creature with huge furry hands and a face like a gorilla's. He caught me before I toppled over, and I remember just screaming and screaming. I was so sure some monster had broken into the house and was going to eat me.

I don't remember much after that, but I did remember mother's arms around me afterwards; soothing, telling me that everything was going to be all right, that no one was going to hurt me. Father and *Achi* and the gorilla were standing in the living room and looking worriedly down at me. The gorilla looked embarrassed.

"I'm sorry," He said, and his voice sounded exactly like Howie-J's. "I'm afraid I get that a lot."

Father used my fright as an excuse to ignore Howie-J after that ("Not good enough. That's not even a real *name*," he had said to mother.), and the rest of dinner was spent with him pretending that *Achi*'s boyfriend wasn't there at all, and *Achi* pointedly talking to Howie-J the whole time, shooting furious looks back at father every now and then.

Afterwards, I went up to my room and found my dictionary. Ignoring father and *Achi* fighting downstairs, I read that a sasquatch was a large primate and, until recently, a legendary creature with a pronounced ridge and features similar to those of an ape's.

Gary was still having some trouble attaching the nose to his face. I wasn't sure if offering to get him some Mighty Bond was a polite or rude thing to do, but after a minute or so of pressing it against the hole under his eyes, Gary slowly took his hand away, and the nose remained in place.

I breathed a sigh of relief, and watched as Gary began to pick at his plate. Mother made sure that none of the meat she served him was bloody enough to make a big mess, but I could smell how raw it was even from where I sat.

Gary crammed a piece of cow into his mouth and chewed methodically ("in a regular and systematic manner"). Something red trickled down his chin. Even father was having trouble eating after seeing that, but he was doing his best not to let it show.

*Achi*'s last and final ex-boyfriend was Gilgamesh, and out of all her boyfriends he was probably the one that father disliked the most. Either *Achi* knew that this was going to happen, or maybe because she was tired of trying to convince father to like her boyfriends, but she and Gilgamesh dated for more than a year before he found out about it. Father flew into a rage soon after.

"I forbid you to date that *hwana!*" I overheard him yelling one night. "I'll disinherit you!"

Father was always threatening to disinherit *Achi* whenever they started arguing about her boyfriends. He never did, but I was sometimes worried, because you never know with father.

"How can you not like him? You haven't even met him yet!" *Achi* yelled back.

"He's a *Saudi!*"

"No, he's not! He's from Iraq! He's been working for Greenpeace for the past sixty years!"

"He isn't even Chinese!"

"He's two-thirds god!"

"Being Chinese is still better than being just two-thirds god and *Arabo!*"

"I'm twenty seven years old! I can date whomever I want!"

"Not as long as you live in my house!"

Things went downhill from there. Gilgamesh was never invited for dinner like all of *Achi*'s other exes, and I was disappointed because I never met an almost-deity ("supernatural being often a central figure of worship") before. That didn't matter to *Achi*. She dated her two-thirds god for one more year until he left for Nepal to build an orphanage there, and it took six more months after that for mother to get them on speaking terms with one another. Father's version of apologizing was to volunteer to arrange a *kai-shao* for *Achi*, because father never really apologizes. I think *Achi* only agreed because she was sick of fighting with father.

"Have some more fried tofu, Gary," Mother said lightly, pushing the plate in his direction.

"Gary can't eat other kinds of food anymore, mom," *Achi* said sourly. "Just raw food."

I tried to imagine how the insides of a zombie could process raw meat. And then I pushed my plate away, because I had officially lost my appetite.

"Would you like some water instead, Gary?" Mother asked blithely. "I'm afraid George has said very little about you... what kind of job do you do again?"

Gary began to make odd, inarticulate ("hard to understand or comprehend") noises. Gary wasn't much of a talker, but I don't think it was from lack of trying. Out of the corner of my eye I saw his mouth move, the flesh around the corners of his lips wrinkling and tearing a little, and then I saw the waxy skin flakes breaking off and drifting down onto the tablecloth. Some more guttural ("sounding harsh to the sense of hearing") sounds were forming out of his throat, but nothing of what he was saying made much sense to me.

Mother also looked a little puzzled, so *Achi* translated. "He's a systems engineer for IBM. He studied Management Engineering and Computer Science in UP. He took a sabbatical ("a specified period for rest") for three years after the automobile accident until his body was fully reanimated, or he would have been senior engineer by now."

"That sounds so difficult," Mother marveled.

"The both of you must be connecting very well," Father said, smiling satisfactorily. "Since you can already understand everything he says, Marcie. Been told it takes awhile to get used to it. And both from UP!"

I disagreed with father, though I made sure not to say it aloud. I think that I would never get used to zombies, even if I could understand what they say.

"I knew what he was saying because I had a lot of zombie friends in college," *Achi* said. "I had practice." I thought she was being a little rude to Gary too, but I don't think Gary was in a condition to care.

Father ignored her. He always did when she was trying to make a point. "I'm very glad Marcie invited you over for dinner, Gary. You're a nice guy, just like your father. I hope we'll be seeing more of you soon."

*Achi* shuddered quietly, but no one else noticed.

She escorted Gary out once dinner was over, much to father's disappointment. "He's got early work the next day," she said, though I could tell that she was lying and that she just wanted Gary out of the house as soon as possible. I relaxed as soon as he was gone. This was the first dinner I'd been in where *Achi*'s boyfriend (though technically, I told myself, Gary was not *Achi*'s boyfriend) was invited and nobody yelled at anybody else. I couldn't help but feel bad for *Achi*, though. Even large, intimidating ("to give off a threatening countenance") Howie-J was handsome when compared to what was left of Gary's face.

I overheard father congratulating himself in the living room afterwards. "He's going to make a suitable son-in-law," he said approvingly. "I can see him inheriting the business one day."

"You didn't ask Marcie what she thought of him," mother began, but father waved away Marcie's thoughts with a wave of his hand.

"She'll come around, naturally. She's thirty years old, Ann, she'll give in soon enough...there's the question of having children of course, but Fred says they've done some successful inseminations in America...we can always fly there and get the treatments needed for Marcie to conceive."

I padded quietly up the stairs, and saw *Achi* coming out of her room. She was wearing a small, secret smile on her lips.

"I hope you don't marry Gary," I told her sincerely. I did not want to have a decomposing zombie for a brother-in-law.

"No chance of that," *Achi* said. "I'm still dating Gilgamesh; it's a long-distance clandestine relationship, and I didn't want father to know." She gestured downstairs. "I talk to him online everyday, and we're going to get married when he comes back to the Philippines in six months. Gary will be a good cover for us until then. I'll break it to them gently once we're married; he won't like it, but he won't be able to do much about it once it's legal." *Achi* lifted a finger to her lips. "Don't tell anyone, all right?"

Still smiling, she headed downstairs.

I stayed standing there for awhile, thinking. I thought about *ho-we*s and *hwana*s and *kai-shao*s. I thought about father and *Achi*, both so convinced that they're right and that the other was wrong. I wondered if I would be married at twenty-five like *Sa-chi*, or twenty-seven at *Di-chi*, or if I will still be unmarried at thirty years old like *Achi*, fighting with father for the right to choose my boyfriends. Or if maybe I'll still be unmarried when I am forty, or fifty, or sixty years old, and if that would still be all right. I don't know.

I went back to my room. I wanted to find out what 'clandestine' meant.

KRISTINE ONG MUSLIM *is the author of* We Bury the Landscape *(Queen's Ferry Press) and several chapbooks, most recently* Insomnia *(Medulla Publishing). Her short fiction and poetry have appeared in over five hundred publications, received three Honorable Mentions in* Year's Best Fantasy and Horror, *and garnered multiple nominations for the Pushcart Prize, Dzanc* Books' Best of the Web 2011, *and the Science Fiction Poetry Association's Dwarf Stars Award and Rhysling Award. She also twice won Sam's Dot Publishing's James Baker Award for Genre Poetry.* Connotation Press *recently nominated one of her short tales for the* storySouth 2012 Million Writers Award. Her work has been published and anthologized in many fine places, including Boston Review, Existere, Narrative Magazine, Southword, The Pedestal Magazine, *and hundreds of genre venues, from* Abyss & Apex *to* One Buck Horror.

# The Chinese Zodiac

## Kristine Ong Muslim

### THE RAT

"They will work for success."

THE *UGLINESS* STARTED off with a warning: that telltale tic in the left eye. Then the rest of the face followed, like an avalanche of flesh. When Nigel finally mustered enough courage to look at his reflection on the mirror, whatever grimace he could conjure resulted in little pools of melted flesh dripping on his feet.

"You still alive in there?" Rachel, the wife, called out, rapping on the locked bathroom door.

"I'll be out in a sec," Nigel replied as if there was nothing wrong. A portion of his lower lip came undone with the effort to speak.

He smiled to her when he opened the bathroom door. All traces of ugliness were now invisible. She was in front of the dresser, checking her make-up.

It was Monday. The office phones rang and rang. The temps down the hall made little effort to silence them.

The division boss, Arnold, strolled past Nigel's cubicle, winked when their eyes met. His golfing hand swished like a celery stalk bereft of its bloody mary. Nigel noticed the blood under Arnold's fingertips. It was the same hand Arnold had used to fondle Nigel in the backroom a month ago, the same hand which had signed off Nigel's promotion terms and those of the ones before him.

Every morning after the day he was promoted, Nigel watched the ugliness taking over. First, his face, and soon, his lower extremities. Fortunately, it disappeared whenever there were people around.

### THE OX
"Only in old age will they find happiness."

LIKE ANY SUCCESSFUL fortune teller before her who is about to give the bad news, she begins slowly, slurs on every ninth syllable. There are no crystal balls in sight. Those were crass; her mother advised her to embrace what's contemporary, to act as if she knew what she was doing. "I see a tall man who had rough hands, an industrial kitchen.... hmm, a soft glimmer of table lamps. Possibly a classy restaurant. He would have been a cook, Miss Gina. He would be hardworking."

Miss Gina conceals her excitement, thinks about the good-looking maitre d' in the Orange Colonnade in SM City. "Does this mean we are going to end up together?" Miss Gina gasps.

The fortune teller takes the money with her right hand before she answers.

### THE TIGER
"Cruel and traitorous."

IT WAS MISCHA'S turn to die.

Her husband and wide-eyed eight-year old children, the identical twins named Wendy and Kate, waited for her to make the first move and take the simmering poisoned chowder into her mouth.

On the opposite corner of the dinner table, Victor smiled to encourage her. He tried not to think of what the twins would have in store for him two days from now.

"You can do it, Mommy," Kate said.

"Yeah," Wendy chimed in, her eyes glowing when it caught the glare of the overhead table lamp. "Remember Uncle Des, he tried to cheat us and pretended that he was already dead so we had to burn him. It was messy, and it hurt him a lot, but his screams made the mess worth it."

Just like before, there was no threat in Wendy's voice, but Mischa could not help but shudder. Years ago, some of her family members did not go down easily, but every one of them was killed in the end. Last night, Mischa thought of running away. How it would be easy to just slip silently out of bed, grab her purse, drive like hell to the airport or the train station, and never look back. But she knew that the twins would eventually find her. Just like Des. And Martha. And Stan. *All of us.*

"Evil," her sister-in-law, Martha, said to her five days after the twins came for her. Mischa remembered how Martha sounded on the phone. Martha asked her to murder her own children. "Des had read this old journal, you know. He said that there was a way out of this. There must be something that will kill the children for good!"

"They've been here before us, Martha, long before our great great grandparents were born." Mischa said. "How could you kill *something* like that?"

Before her sat the bowl of chowder. It was growing cold.

"Please don't make us hurt you, Mommy," Kate said.

Victor was not looking at her.

Wendy smiled at her and took her twin sister's hand.

## THE RABBIT

"They create romance amidst a dreary life."

Sylvia insisted that the man who had brought her the white roses came from a spot on the kitchen's linoleum floor.

"He just materialized from out of nowhere, Jude. You have to believe me," she said to her younger sister, Judith, over the phone. "It was scary at first. But then he smiled and told me that he only wanted to give me the flowers. Then he melted off after that, melted away...down the floor, Jude. As if he never existed. But I still have the flowers. They're right here on the countertop."

Judith did not say anything.

"They're beautiful, Jude."

JUDITH HAD A key to her sister's place. The twins had been roommates since college until Judith moved out two years ago to live with her husband and one-year old son.

When Judith entered the foyer of Sylvia's apartment, she saw the white flowers propped like sentinels on a clear glass vase at the center of the coffee table.

Sylvia smiled at her from her place in the couch, a magazine on her lap.

"Hi, Jude. I heard the door lock click. I knew it was you."

Without bothering to sit down, Judith placed her purse on an easy chair near the television set and said: "You need to see a doctor, Syl. Just talk to someone, I mean, maybe it's because of those migraine medications you were taking."

"Listen, Jude—"

"You need help, Syl. I know you would hate me for saying that. But a man growing out of the floor, some sort of an admirer who brings you flowers! Christ!"

"You might not believe it, but it wasn't like I was hallucinating or something. It was so real, Jude. I could even see the creases on his shirt as if he had slept on the clothes he was wearing."

Judith finally broke down with nervous laughter, the kind one usually did during a game of Russian roulette the moment the trigger clicked and the bullet was just a chamber away, and everybody on the table knew who among the players would not go home that night.

"I know," Sylvia said, laughing now. "It does sound crazy. But I don't care."

ENTERING HER APARTMENT door, Sylvia took off her gray coat and deposited her keys on the coffee table where an issue of *Scientific American* was opened to page 32—the article about the neutrino, that subatomic particle which could not be detected.

On the hardwood table she had purchased from a flea market, the green bud vase containing a plastic orange flower looked out of place among the jumble of hardbound books, DVDs, and three decorative lamps she had bought before she realized that she had nowhere else to place them.

One could not look at an angle of her apartment without seeing one lamp. Lampshades—colorful ones, delicate ones, somber ones, ornate Oriental-inspired ones complete with ceramic rabbits—they lingered like children bottled up with their candies and security blankets, all warmth and contentment so that they could only give out a soft, silent glow.

She turned on the kitchen TV, flicked the remote control. *Constantine* on HBO. On Cinemax, the ethereal Anthony Hopkins grinned at her from the screen. Then she stopped scrolling when she chanced upon the Discovery Channel jingle, the "I love the whole world" litany. Had to listen to that one in its entirety. Had to believe its inevitable simplicity. She finally decided on Foxcrime with its documentary about a serial killer in a sleepy small town in South Carolina.

She turned her attention to the fridge and took out a bar of cheese, a bundle of asparagus stalks from the crisper, and the container of leftover baked potatoes. She ate slices of cheese while waiting for the asparagus to cook on the skillet she had drizzled with olive oil and finely chopped tomatoes, glancing at the television screen once in a while. Doing the nightly inventory, she took note of her dwindling supply of onions and bananas and how the small fluorescent bulb on the kitchen sink was showing signs of being burnt out.

In the corner, the covered trash can was filled to the brim and had to be emptied. *Tomorrow,* Sylvia noted.

She switched to the local news and tried, at least, to pay attention to the news anchor and her perfectly made up face. *The lighting was bad, though,* she thought. So was the weather.

Outside, the rain was not showing any signs of letting up.

She waited for the man to show up.

When he finally materialized on that same spot on the kitchen's linoleum floor, he was still anchored from the knees down.

## THE DRAGON
### "They rarely give true love."

EVERYBODY IN THE hall wanted to take a whiff of the bath robe Marilyn Monroe wore as she lay dying.

A towel with intricate embroidery of bleeding heart vines was draped ceremoniously on her face. There was blood on the collar near her slashed jugular, and the smell had been exquisite. Her underwear was soiled. Candle wax curdled inside her left ear canal. Stainless steel S&M paraphernalia at the bottom drawer of the bedside table. These details were not in the news until now.

The police gave me hot chocolate and Danish pastry for showing up early. I took all the necessary photographs and divulged nothing until I was offered enough money by the Free Press.

I confessed that the location of the first slaughterhouse was still a secret. And that the most beautiful women in the world died the same deaths as the rest of us. The envy they stirred in us kept us entertained, kept us wishing for their suffering not to end lest we begin to notice ours, kept us exhaling all these beautiful curses behind their backs.

## THE SNAKE
### "They possess wisdom and jealousy."

GEORGE FOSTER HAD never looked more comfortable than the way he slumped on the purple couch, with his mouth hanging open. The curtains were blown inwardly by the faint breeze as if to keep his soul (or whatever it was that he had inside that husk of him).

George had a special look of dying that made his wife, Frances, want to kill him again and again. It was the look of an unconquerable man who would say: "You see, Frances, I will always be alive whether you like it or not."

She rearranged him many times over so he would *remain* dead to her. That was how things should be: when someone died, he should not keep on looking as if he was only relaxing on his front porch while sipping a glass of lemonade. After all, George had been a good husband. It did not matter if he could not keep his hands off his neighbor's little girl. George never screamed at her, never beat her like Jennifer Lemay's husband did, and never cheated on her with other women.

The little girls were another story.

The day after Frances had slipped him the antifreeze-laden miso soup, she still set the table for two and brought him white tea, the expensive kind, on his self-appointed place on the couch. Just like before, he still said no to the tea.

When George started to stink, Frances aired out the house every night.

## THE HORSE
### "Superficial and flamboyant."

I REMEMBERED THAT when I made the world, I never attempted to recreate reality; I simply wanted to deface it.

Maybe that was why nobody paid attention when I arrived for the third time and declared that I was the Messiah, except maybe for a handful of religious fanatics who had a penchant for good old mail-order holy water, sacred stones, and clay effigies. Everyone thought that I was a madman, and a doctor gave me a prescription for antidepressants. When I walked on water and parted the Pacific Ocean, I was given an hour of live worldwide telecast via satellite. My feat was not even deemed primetime material.

There was no need for me to heal the sick for it was already the twenty-fourth century A.D., and diseases were very rare. The only things that humans worried about were psychological disorders and boredom. As for food, it was abundant with the advent of synthetic production of vegetables, white worms, and "sweet" meat (which was nothing but digested cellulose with ground beef flavor). Crime was a luxury, and everyone spent half their allotted lifetime watching TV.

This decadent world touched me on a spiritual level; I started to worship what I could never become in the eyes of the people I had created in my likeness.

I exhibited stigmata when I let blood pour out endlessly from holes in my wrists and feet. Somebody injected me with a powerful coagulant, and the blood clotted, the superficial wounds healed.

I spoke in all languages. A four year old answered me in Aramaic and poked fun at me.

I simulated the burning bush of infinite wisdom. I got doused by a milligram of fire retardant.

I called out the Plagues and the Furies, but the people had portable Dyson Spheres™ and unshakable immune systems.

There was nothing else to do. Miracles were a nineteenth-century fad, and this generation was motivated only by entertainment. Awe and fear could only be inspired by wrestling shows in zero gravity and the effects of relativistic length contraction on a lab rat hurtled to light speed.

In a way, what *my* people evolved into made me feel like a proud parent. They were indifferent and self-sufficient. They did not need souls. And with quantum mechanics, they did not even have to actually *exist* before they could live.

Next time, I would create them using natural means: out of a kiln and baked until well done and never medium rare so that their lifetime would be reduced to ten years. Might make them easier to control.

## The Sheep
"They are timid and worry so much."

WE CALL YOU *Goliath*. That may be your real name. Like Sting or Madonna.

You have wasted so much time thinking about what you must do. Now, the crowd whispers about you. You hear the word *slow*. Somebody says *lump of meat*. You probably want to talk back: *just because I'm big doesn't mean I'm slow, but Mama has told me to never talk to strangers.*

The women huddle, laughing among themselves. So many eyes. You do not know which way is out.

Below is a little guy, gloating. No bigger than your fore-arm, and he's screaming from a loud horn about your mama being a *beetch*—a word you associate to a "dog's mama." You do not understand what your mother has to do with the ruckus. You only want to ask them for the way home.

The little guy has a makeshift slingshot that looks like pantyhose. He dangles it, and everybody cheers. They call him *Daaeyveed*. You see the stone in his hand. You want to cheer for him, too. Perhaps, they'll let you in on the game if you cheer.

You say: "DAAEYVEED!" The children wet their pants, half of the women pass out, and the men draw their swords.

Then the little guy called Daaeyveed swings his pantyhose contraption and aims the stone straight into your eye.

Brushing the dirt away from your eye, you stagger and step on something slippery. You go down. A volcano explodes in another town. Earthquakes ripple across the continent. You realize that you have crashed down onto two generations of townspeople who have been howling for your demise.

It is only an accident, but history books keep on saying it's *genocide*.

## THE MONKEY
### "Cunning and selfish."

I USED TO be a miller before my daughter met that little man named Rumpelstiltskin. Luck and common sense had it in for me, so when the tavern folks bragged about their exploits from foreign lands, all the monsters they claimed to vanquish, the many wives they supposedly stored inside their closets, and how they make room for new ones by piling one corpse on top of the other, I had no choice but to proclaim the biggest lie of all: that my daughter could spin straw into gold. Never mind that the twit had her mother's penchant for Harlequin Romances where bosoms heaved and everybody sleeps around. You see, I loved my daughter. I wanted her to achieve what no bimbo her age could accomplish. When I heard that the king was interested in

# ERVE FILES

## CROSSLISTING: _____

_____     _____

r Copy     Docutek Web     Innopac Web**

*ermine which formats will be the most beneficial to your course.*

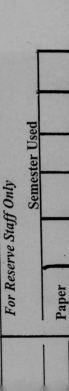

*For Reserve Staff Only*

Semester Used

Paper

marrying a girl half his age provided she could spin straw into precious metal, well, I guess I was vindicated.

## THE ROOSTER
"Narrow-minded and vain."

ON THE THIRD day, when the hounds of hell had finally missed them, she helped Russell to his grave. She made sure that all the preparations for his second coming were done by the book.

Sella sloughed off his skin with a blunt knife.

The pain was killing Russell, but he wanted to understand the purpose of this suffering better than anyone.

"What are you going to do with my skin?" He looked away from the exposed flesh of his chest.

"I'll sew you a coat," Stella explained. "One that will let you hide your rot underneath."

Together, they went out to the world above.

## THE DOG
"Faithful, lacks stability."

SOMETHING THAT WAS very clichéd had to happen sometimes, and Alden fell in love.

"Let me try again to put you back together," he said to Evvie.

So he grasped a portion of air in his left hand and another with his right hand. Evvie, a forgotten part of her, should be caught in these swirling packets of air after her family scattered her ashes in this farmland.

Alden brought his hands closer to his face and inhaled what he imagined would be Evvie. And just like before, nothing happened. Not even a silent intake of breath, a sound at the end of a couplet written in blank verse.

*You're crazy,* was what his sister said. She thought it was ridiculous, even laughable, the idea of Alden prowling, ducking to make sure no one noticed him every weekend at the farmland owned by Evvie's stepfather. Then she saw something in Alden's eyes, and it made her uneasy. *Please, Alden, promise me you'll stop this madness, okay? Evvie didn't even know you exist. You're that pimply little kid nobody ever noticed. Remember what she called you when we were still in grade school? While her beautiful circle of friends gathered around you like you're some sort of carnival freak let loose in the hallway? Why do you have this stupid, stupid obsession?* There, there, she was finally able to tell her little brother the truth. That should show him and breathe sense in his tortured little head.

When Alden said nothing and she still saw the same light in his eyes, she decided to tell their parents when they got home that night. She did not care if Alden would be grounded for life, as long as he would forget about that evil twit cheerleader-my-ass girl of his dreams.

Five years later, Alden was still trying to put back Evvie together by gathering the ashes that she had left. Even if he had brought her to life once again, he still did not expect Evvie to love him back. Besides, *that* did not matter to Alden.

And everywhere he went, he could smell the air that contained all the pieces that Evvie had left for him to inhale.

## THE PIG
"Whenever they play pranks on others,
they will never know when to stop."

TERRANCE SOMETIMES IMAGINED a life, a different one, one where he was not supposed to see and understand what had happened to *them.*

He adjusted the rear view mirror again to make sure that there was nobody in the backseat peering at him and trying to catch a ride. Some roadkill, perhaps. Some hit-and-run victim who never found his way home, who was left to die in a forgotten back road, who had been calling for help on the same spot on the road where his blood had long ago been washed away after his body had been wheeled inside the morgue.

A family van, luggage swaying on top of it like the head of a giant mechanical pineapple, moved past him. From the passenger window, a boy stuck out his tongue to him, showing the blue gob of a chewing gum.

Terrance winked at the boy.

The car stereo was playing Pink Floyd's *Hey You* when the bass lines began to dissolve into static.

Terrance fiddled with the tuner. It was the best part of the song.

*Bad reception,* he thought. *Must be these hills.*

One by one, he tried the other frequencies until he hit the jackpot. Live's *Overcome.* He smiled.

When he turned his attention to the road again, he caught sight of a girl in a yellow dress. Waving at him, she stood by the left side of the road. Her stare was coaxing him to stop, to invite her in. She seemed lost and pitiful. The trees swarmed above her, and the lonely stretch of the road, the endless highway with its dust and grit and indifference, made her look small.

"No," he whispered.

He knew she could hear him even through the roar of wind against the glass. All of them did. All the loneliest, angriest sounds in the universe they produced, and he always said no. They were beyond help.

Speeding past her, he was not surprised that the girl was no longer on that spot of the road when he looked back.

Four miles ahead, Terrance spotted her again. She was beckoning to him beside the electric post. Her hunched form now had an air of desperation.

The wind behind her stirred the dust, sending clouds of it everywhere. It did not ruffle her hair, and the hem of her yellow dress remained very, very still.

When the car got near her, he noticed a slash of red at her side and that her dress was torn and was only held together by her tiny left hand, the right hand still waving for him to stop, for him to take a look at what had become of her, for him to care.

"I'm sorry," he said, not looking back. "I'm so sorry."

It had already started to rain when he reached the city. All the vermin that nobody could see stirred in their sleepless haunts. Terrance felt their eyes study him from every street corner, heard them wailing from the underground sewers where some of them had been trapped. They each hold a piece of the dark city in their hands—what was left of their hands.

Isa *was born in 1990. She studied for two years in Ateneo de Manila University, and served as the English Editor for* Heights, *before transferring to Santa Clara University in California, where she is currently finishing a degree in Marketing. Her work has been published in* Heights, The Philippine Star, The Philippines Free Press, Diaspora Ad Astra, Philippine Speculative Fiction, *volumes IV, V, and the forthcoming volume VII. She likes dogs with smashed noses, fairytales, and poems that include references to the skeletal structure.*

# Pure

## Isabel Yap

HANNAH THOUGHT IT was just a temporary thing. A Boylet Thing, which her pretty friends tended to go through—someone they met in Tagaytay over the weekend, who was handsome and charming then turned out to be a distant relative; a cute guy at the gym who was the next up-and-coming-artista and had too many fans for it to be anything but futile. A lot of the time it seemed to be mostly in their heads: a glance, a comment that could be thought of as friendly *but was hopefully something more*.

Hannah preferred it this way. It was one of those half-true jokes that she was their *barkada*'s Mother Hen. The type their parents called when they went out to the mall. The one who got best in conduct at school. The person who sniffed out potential suitors and smiled frozenly at them when they were Clearly Not Okay.

From their high school gang of six, three of them had gone to the same college as Hannah: Ria, who loved computers and marathoned pirated DVDs; Kim, who used to run until she damaged her knees and now spent half her time painting; and Arrie, their naïve little baby, who had somehow turned out to be the dude-magnet. They tried to have lunch together twice a week, and it was four weeks into college that Arrie cheerfully proclaimed she had *kwento*.

"So this guy, Lance," Arrie started. She was smiling in that shy, slightly foreboding way that Hannah both loved and hated. She and Arrie had gotten really close in third grade, after some stroke of fate had made them seatmates. They had been in elementary and high school choir together, but while Arrie joined their college acapella group, Hannah decided not to try out, in order to survive the Pre-Med course she had somehow worked up the guts to take. Hannah loved Arrie, though she had a tendency to be a little too sweet. Clingy was the word Hannah did *not* want to use on her best friend. She raised her eyebrows expectantly, so Arrie continued, "He's in choir. And in my Lit class and my Econ class."

"And you like him," Hannah deadpanned.

Arrie shifted in her seat. "As a friend," she demurred. Which clearly meant just the opposite.

LANCE TURNED OUT to be an incredibly fresh, smiley, soccer-player-slash-tenor, and not actually a total stranger. They had met before at those large family-friend gatherings that Hannah's parents used to insist she attend. She remembered being at the kids' table, where everyone sat around awkwardly eating their noodles or punching away at their Gameboy Colors. Lance might have been one of the chattier boys, but she couldn't place him in particular.

Arrie thought this was great news. She squeezed Hannah's arm afterwards. "So you know his parents!"

"My parents know his parents," Hannah corrected. In order not to sound too unenthusiastic, she added, "He seems nice."

He *did*, although the fact that he was all Arrie wanted to talk about these days was exhausting, and took the shine out of him more than anything else. He seemed too cheerful, too easy to talk to, too eager to please. Hannah began to feel that she and Lance had a mutual, cordial dislike for each other. Sometimes he'd have lunch with them, and sometimes Hannah, Kim, and Ria would thoughtfully leave, saving their giggles until they had gone past the cafeteria doors.

That's what it was—something to laugh at, some gossip to discuss when they were sick of complaining about how much they were drowning in school work, which was mostly true (never mind the fact that they were freshmen and this was the *easy* part). The day Arrie and Lance walked into the cafeteria holding hands, their table stood up and clapped. Hannah decided this was going just fine, nothing to worry about.

Or it was, until the day Arrie took Hannah to the library for help with Chemistry ("Because you know I'm hopeless with the periodic table!") and then started weeping over her notes, blotting some of the ink. Hannah put her hand over her friend's shoulder and steered her to the bathroom, where she listened to the tearful confession: "His parents. They want us to split. They want him to date a pure Chinese girl. He says he can't do anything to change their minds!"

It had been about two months of peace, Hannah speculated. She should have seen this coming earlier. Her parents had been of a similar opinion until her *kuya* married an incredibly sweet Ilocana and procured them a lovely grandchild. Their arguments about his former girlfriends had been catastrophic; many of them still rang loudly in her ears. Arrie had been one of the few non-Chinese-Filipinos in their high school batch; her Mandarin was passable, but she could never be mistaken as otherwise. Lance probably knew this was coming, but Arrie could charm her way whenever she wanted to—he probably couldn't help himself. Hannah decided it was worth trying to salvage what they could.

"You weren't officially together yet," she started, trying for soothing. "Wait it out. Take it slow. Don't make it seem like it worries you too much."

"We were almost—officially together—as good as!" Arrie sniffled.

"If he really likes you, he'll sort it out," Hannah answered. She was starting to sound stern, which was no good, but she couldn't *help* it.

"But they won't *let* him like me!"

"They could change their minds." She was trying to steer herself back into soothing. "Remember my *kuya*? It'll be fine."

"I don't think so," Arrie sobbed. Hannah knew it was wrong of her, but she silently agreed.

IT DIDN'T TAKE too long for the others to find out, and they called for a sleepover that weekend, despite everyone's crammed schedules. Arrie needed cheering up. They ate Dairy Queen for dessert after gorging themselves on sushi, then went over to Ria's house and laughed over a bunch of YouTube videos featuring unusually violent Japanese game shows. Then, when they were all trying to fight the first wave of sleepiness, Arrie again wondered aloud what she could do.

Ria came up with brilliant idea to do a Google search on it. Perhaps they could find some inspiring stories. They waited, without much hope, as the lists came up. Kim had started to whistle in her sleep. "Check this out," Ria said, and Arrie and Hannah stared at the screen with bleary eyes. It was a badly designed homepage for a specialty store in Binondo, which claimed to make potions. There were cures for stomach ache and nausea, and things like foot creams and callous removers, and then the list got progressively weirder—voice enhancing fluid, overnight nose repair creams, cursing powder—shrinks assets!—for enemies. The English was sketchy, although the prices and ingredients listed beneath each item were oddly meticulous. Near the bottom of the page was the item that had turned up relevant on the Google search: a syrup that *made drinker into being pure Chinese—guaranteed!*

Hannah decided it was 2:00 AM and that they were going to have nightmares if they kept on reading, although Arrie continued to stare at the page for a while, as if it might actually be worth looking into. "That sounds so shady," Hannah loudly proclaimed. "And it's three thousand pesos? What a rip-off."

Arrie nodded distractedly. There was a strange twist to her smile. "It's pretty random, huh? But then why would they claim to have something like that?"

Ria laughed and said she'd print out the page for Arrie if she wanted, and then they *really* had to sleep already, they were going to mass before lunch the next morning. Hannah laughed too; if Arrie wanted to waste her money on a joke, there was no helping that.

HANNAH LIVED WITH Tita Grace, who had a condo closer to campus, and no *yaya* or driver. Her parents wanted her to stay at home, but again the Pre-Med course and the promise of major traffic every afternoon meant that she could have a little freedom. Tita Grace was single, rich, and frugal, an odd combination that meant she was out most nights, extremely overworked, but also rather cheerful. Hannah found herself alone most weekdays, which suited her and her textbooks just fine. She was dozing over her third half-hearted read of the same paragraph when her phone jiggled across the table, the silent mode failing her, as usual. She answered it crossly.

"Hello?"

"Hannah? Hannah! It's me." The voice on the other end was quavery and crackling. Hannah couldn't place it. She moved to the window to get better reception.

"Hello? Who's this?"

"It's Arrie," the voice said, but there was something pleading about it, as if it wasn't really sure. "Hannah, please, I need your help." Hannah stared at the clock across the room. It was just about to become Sunday morning. Since their sleepover Arrie had been pretty quiet about the issue, though she had left their table to meet up with Lance twice that week. Hannah had hoped they were working through it.

"Arrie? Where are you? What's wrong?"

"I'm on my way. I'm taking a taxi. I need to stay at your place for a while."

"What? Why?" Tita Grace wouldn't mind, and Hannah was fine with it, but the desperation in her friend's voice was making her worry. "Arrie, what happened?"

"I did it—" she answered. "I bought the thing from that potions store. It worked, Hannah, it really did!" She sounded completely joyful for a moment, then her voice took on that low, desperate tone again. "But I can't stay at home right now—I'll tell you everything later, I'm really near. I'll call you again when I'm outside." She ended the call before Hannah could say anything else.

THE SECOND CALL came as promised, though it didn't go at all the way Hannah had imagined—Arrie had argued with her parents, maybe because she had spent her allowance on something so stupid; she had left home in a moment of craziness because the issue was reaching its breaking point in Arrie's mind. Hannah had cleared out the books piled on the second guest room's desk, which she sometimes used as a study. She made sure there was toilet paper in the bathroom and was wondering how best to explain to Tita Grace when her phone buzzed in her pocket.

"I'm standing outside your unit. Hannah, I swear it's me, but I look kinda different. Please, please—don't freak out when you open the door."

The room suddenly seemed a little chilly. It was a strange thing to say, and Hannah knew Arrie *wasn't* crazy. But it *was* incredibly early in the morning, and still dark outside. She walked to the door and found herself looking out through the rarely used peephole, listening to Arrie's breathing on the line.

The stranger standing outside had her mobile phone against her ear. She was wearing Arrie's favorite shirt—a black graphic tee from Zara that they had collectively picked out for her the year before—and seemed to be about Arrie's height, but her creamy skin and deep black eyes seemed ghostly, her smile in the yellow lamp light too tiny, pressed at the corners. Hannah stepped back, closed her eyes, shook her head. She returned to the door, looked through the peephole, saw the smile faltering on the girl's face, heard the sudden stream of anxious chatter in her ear:

"We were walking through the park in first year and got chased by those dogs and you threw a stone at it that got lodged in its eye and you never told the owner; you have a mole right above your belly button and you hate it and I only saw it because I accidentally went into the room once when you were changing; you're scared of Toni Braxton's *Unbreak My Heart* and hearing it used to give you nightmares as a kid—"

She watched the words come out of the foreign girl's mouth. They were all things only Arrie could know, but what convinced Hannah above all else was that tearful note that only her friend could conjure, that got Hannah to give in even at the worst of times, because she knew Arrie was pure and kind and needed protecting in the way most of her friends no longer did. She twisted the door open and let the girl come inside. Arrie started to cry as she leaned in for an embrace, even as Hannah murmured into her shoulder, "What the hell have you *done*?"

SHE DECIDED THAT Arrie had to stay in her room that night, and thanked her luck while Arrie was taking a shower that she didn't have classes until the afternoon the next day. They curled up together on Hannah's bed and she listened, still half wondering if this wasn't a bizarre nightmare, to how Arrie had gone to Binondo and found the store, wedged between slippers and SLR cameras. How the owner had been overly enthusiastic, describing cases like hers that had worked out great.

How she had taken the potion crouched on her bathtub's edge; how it burned her throat on its way down, and it took only a few moments before she felt her insides burning up, was conscious of her blood thrumming through her veins, the hot sensation like flames—how she lifted her hands up to her face, watching her skin turn paler, seeing her face shift smaller and more delicate, her eyes turning into shimmering buttons. She was utterly convinced that her blood had been altered.

"And? Is it permanent?"

Arrie pressed her face against her pillow with what sounded like a moan.

Hannah felt something twist inside her. "Is it?"

"I have to meet his parents within three days. That's the condition. Or—or it won't quite—I'll go back to the way I've always been, and it would be such a waste." She sat upright, and seized Hannah's sleeve. "Hannah, you *have* to help me. I can't be without him. I love him. He told me—he told me last Tuesday that he wasn't sure what to do about it—it sounded like he wanted us to go see other people, but I *need him*."

Hannah stared at the bright, frantic look in Arrie's eyes, and once again felt that sudden sensation of iciness in her chest. But it would be useless to say anything, not now, not anymore. She knew no one else would believe Arrie—not even Ria or Kim, who did not share the years of friendship *they* did—so until this was over, she was the only one who could do anything about it. Thankfully, it was a hell week at school; three days of being too busy to deal with the others would not be amiss. She took Arrie's hand and pressed it between both of hers. "I'll do what I can," she promised.

BUT LANCE WAS not Hannah's friend, and had never talked to her when Arrie was not around. It was pointless for Arrie to attend her classes—the teacher would notice her and wonder what she was doing there—so she told Hannah she would try and wait to talk to Lance after his classes. Hannah rushed to find them after taking her Psych midterms—she finished it in half the allotted time—and worried what Lance would think of this new girl's hungry eyes, the way she seemed to think she knew him.

She caught them by the empty classroom where they usually lingered before the next period, in time to see Lance backing away from the door. "You're crazy," he was saying, and Hannah saw a single bead of sweat tracing down the side of his head. "Where's Arrie? What did you do to her?"

"It's me, I'm her," Arrie sobbed. "Remember—we sang that song for freshie night—"

Lance turned his head and caught Hannah standing there. She moved forward, reaching out a hand to snatch at his wrist—"Lance, wait!" but he had already shaken his head and jogged away, just as a group of students were emerging from down the hall. Hannah started to run after him, but Arrie stopped her with a broken, quiet "Don't."

THE NEXT DAY Lance was not at school. When Hannah suggested that they go to his house, Arrie shook her head violently and said that it was against the rules; he *had* to bring her there himself. Arrie tried texting him, then calling. Hannah was not really surprised when he did not reply. By this time she had half a mind to tear him apart—maybe even if it would hurt Arrie in the process. Then she realized, with a sickened feeling, that the damage had already been mostly done.

THE THIRD DAY Hannah resolutely missed all her classes and asked Arrie to wait, she was going to try to explain things to Lance herself. Arrie had gotten paler and quieter since she had first arrived. Tita Gracie had accepted Hannah's explanation of a friend whose parents were out of town for the week without any suspicion, although she had pulled Hannah aside to tell her that her friend looked really sick and probably needed to see a doctor. *You just don't know,* Hannah thought, but decided not to be too gloomy about it. If what Arrie said was true, then she'd be back to normal by the end of the day, and that seemed almost a better bargain. She had been avoiding that thought because she knew it would break her friend's heart, but seeing how Lance had acted the last two days had confirmed her opinion that he would never deserve Arrie.

Still, she was going to keep her promise and try.

She asked Arrie to wait for her in the cafeteria while she went to find Lance—Arrie had told her his schedule, but he seemed to be moving out of routine, probably as a way to keep avoiding the girl that had turned up and claimed to be Arrie. She caught him, finally, in that square of gravel behind the library that was meant to be extra parking space but had somehow been ignored by everyone. He was holding the hands of another girl, looking into her eyes, leaning in to press a chaste kiss against her forehead—

"You asshole!" Hannah watched with satisfaction as Lance jolted back, and both he and the girl whipped their heads around to stare at her in horror. "*Three days* and you forget all about her? You thought we wouldn't find out? And *you*—I bet you knew he was already dating someone. Do you really want to go for a guy like that?"

The girl, who looked disconcertingly like the one Arrie had tried to become, flushed red. "I didn't think—" she started.

"Come on," Lance said, seizing the girl's arm and pulling her away. "And if you're talking about Arrie, Hannah, you're wrong. She knew it was over between us. I broke up with her two weeks ago." He stared at her with his brow furrowed for a moment, before turning and walking away.

"Great!" Hannah shouted, her hands curling into fists; she knew her ears were turning red, and was surprised to find that her eyes were starting to burn with angry tears. "Now she won't have to keep kidding herself that a guy like you is worth it!"

She was still fuming when Lance and The Girl rounded the corner to the library—still trying too hard to control her anger that she missed the soft crunch of footsteps behind her, didn't see the girl with nearly translucent skin who was running away, trying in vain to rub her eyes free of tears.

HANNAH FOUND ARRIE in the cafeteria, looking so sunken that she decided it was time to go home. On the way there she was going to have to explain what happened—as delicately as she could, despite the anger that had not fully receded. But when the car engine was running and she tried to start off cautiously with "I found him," Arrie just shook her head and said, "No, forget it, not now, Hannah, please? I think I—I don't want to hear it. I'm going to take a nap, okay?"

Hannah felt sympathetic, but also righteous and irritated, as if this had been a long time coming and maybe they should have both seen it long ago. And if what Lance said was true…but she wasn't going to trust anything that bastard said, and this wasn't the time. "Okay," she answered, and kept her mouth closed.

Arrie smiled at her. "Thanks." She shut her eyes and after a moment was dozing, but Hannah found she kept looking at her friend during lulls in the traffic, trying to make sure she was still breathing, however softly.

HANNAH DIDN'T WONDER at what time the changes would take effect. Maybe she should have acted quicker, thought faster, been more suspicious, kept a clearer head. Arrie had gone into the bathroom for her evening shower, just as the sun was starting to set. It was five minutes before there was a cacophony in the bathroom, like bottles tumbling down, followed by sharp cries of pain. Hannah didn't stop to think—she ran for the door, but of course it was locked; she had to run for the key in Tita Grace's room, shouting behind her shoulder that she was coming in, hold on—

The screams had barely stopped when her trembling hands finally opened the door. Arrie was sprawled half across the tiles and half across the bathroom mat—her skin was practically transparent, the veins showing clean through them; her glassy black eyes had swollen so much they seemed to bulge out of her head; her limbs curled, like they had been bent into unnatural poses and frozen that way.

Hannah knew that she screamed, too—an abrupt one, that she couldn't help—she was repulsed by that thing on the floor but she stooped down to gather it up, the skin and bones, forced herself to stare at those bulging eyes and say, "I'm going to call a doctor, I'm going to get Tita Grace, or let me take you to the hospital, it'll be okay, are you in pain," then her thoughts cascaded into one another and she burst out with, "*Oh my god Arrie you didn't tell me you should have told me oh my god—*"

"Don't, no, don't go anywhere, don't tell anyone, just stay here with me," it—Arrie—(could she even still be called that?) was saying, and it was weeping, huge tears leaking out of those huge, empty eyes, "Just stay here with me, just stay, I'm sorry Hannah," it clung to her, the fingers with veins and bones and muscles exposed clutched at her back and she shuddered but clung to it as well, because what else could she do? "I'm so sorry, Hannah, so sorry..."

IT WAS TWO hours later when Arrie seemed to—fall asleep, maybe. Turn unconscious? The blurred shape of her heart was still beating through her clear-colored chest—and Hannah found herself thinking with perfect clarity that there was only one thing she could try to fix this, as she bundled up Arrie in a robe. She had shriveled further, she seemed to be shrinking, almost deflating, still getting skinnier. Hannah turned on her computer and printed out a page, with steely determination, then stuffed her wallet with all her cash savings. She carried Arrie carefully to the car, shuddering at how she seemed to weigh nothing, made sure the house gate was locked, then set off for Binondo.

The stall was still open. The woman inside it was tiny and bent and never looked up but laughed, in a crackly way, when Hannah tried to explain, in her stilted Fookien, what had happened, caught somewhere between terror, anger, and calm. In fifteen minutes she was walking out of there, the moon winking on her clean-shaven head, because that had been faster than cash. The antidote, unsurprisingly, was also liquid. She was almost certain that it would hurt twice as badly as the first.

She knew it had been Arrie's fault, too, maybe even more than Lance's, more than her own for letting it reach this point. But she couldn't imagine no longer hearing her friend laugh, sing, and talk about the beautiful things that made up her day; her habit of squeezing her eyes shut whenever she was excited; her tendency to wring Hannah's arm and beg her to duet Britney's *Sometimes*, the song they had first bonded over, as seatmates, nine years ago.

She opened the car door, spied the ghostly white shoulder against her peach towel, pressed her fingers against her friend's collarbone. She did not think about how she might have mistranslated the old lady saying it could be too late. Did not think about the way Arrie had cried and apologized, while begging Hannah to stay with her. Why the pleading? Hannah had never left. She was never going to. Unless...

She felt her breath catch. She took hold of Arrie's shoulder, gently, and moved it back and forth. And again, with more pressure, her voice rising above a whisper, to repeat her friend's name, her friend's plea: "Arrie? Arrie?"

CHRISTINE V. LAO*'s stories have appeared in the anthology* Philippine Speculative Fiction *(volumes 5, 6, and 7),* Philippine Genres Stories, *the* Philippines Graphic, *and the* Philippines Free Press. *Her poems have been featured in* Kritika Kultura, *an international refereed electronic journal, and in* Under the Storm: An Anthology of Contemporary Philippine Poetry. *She lists the books she eats for breakfast at christinevlao.blogspot. com.*

# Dimsum

## Christine V. Lao

HE IS A security guard on night watch, a calling that
suits his bulky frame and simple disposition. His charge, The
Garden of the Coming Happiness Tea House: A windowless
room ventilated by slow-whirring ceiling fans, occupying
the ground floor of one of Chinatown's oldest buildings—a
structure so ancient and unreliable that the city government periodically attempts its demolition. It stands today,
still, thanks to the tea house's mob of ravenous customers;
their packed bodies, a wall that every ambitious city official
with an eye toward the mayor's office invariably refuses to
attack.

The tea house is celebrated for its *bao zi*—round, white,
and slightly sweet, bread-like buns steamed in bamboo bas-
kets and filled with barbecued pork; chicken balls and hard-
boiled egg; crab roe and broth; or a variety of sweet paste.
The *bao zi* are so popular that rumors of the tea house using
cat meat as filling have become a beloved urban legend, at-
tracting, rather than repelling, new customers.

There is really nothing much for him to do at the tea house.
Here, everybody means business—that is, everyone comes

to the tea house to satiate that simplest, most elemental desire.

Once, during his early days of employment, a man with a gun—likely a novice—had attempted to rob the tea house. He was beaten to a pulp by the customers, angered by his interruption. The guard had watched without pleasure as the mob turned the gun-toting man into a bloody, mewling creature. It was he who'd called the police when the crowd had returned to its dimsum.

"Happened so fast. No one could stop them," he'd told the men in blue.

"Them?"

"Happened so fast. They're long gone."

After the police had left with the body, he'd run from his post and gagged violently in the alley.

AT THE END of his shift and just before first light, he leaves the tea house through the kitchen door, a bag of *bao zi* carefully hidden underneath his jacket. There are shadows that scurry alongside him as he rapidly traverses the alley. He is on his way to the pharmacy around the corner, where the pharmacist's assistant is busy setting up shop for the day.

They had been sweethearts once, when she was still a student at city college, rail thin and homely, ready to trade her love for a meal. She'd made no secret of her fondness for the tea house's warm *cha siu bao*—steamed pork buns—and because he was always one who made do with what he was given, he'd won her by promising a supply every morning. In return, she'd agreed to live with him, allowed him to pay her tuition with his wages from the tea house.

For a while, it seemed, love bloomed, nurtured by the *bao zi* surreptitiously snatched from the tea house kitchen, or rescued from the pile destined for the garbage bin (the chef was a tyrant who demanded perfection: every *bao*, a smooth, firm half-dome exactly ten cm in diameter). But she quickly grew tired of her favorite meat-filled *bao zi*, and cajoled him to bring home other items on the menu.

And bring them home, he did: The delicately flavored *tsai pao*, of crunchy beansprouts, imported dark green vegetables, and Sichuan pickles; the exotic *zhi ma bao zi*, perfectly white and round on the outside, but oozing with black sesame paste on the inside; its less adventurous cousin, the *dou sha bao zi*, a fluffy mound injected with crushed sweet bean slurry; the fragrant *lian rong bao* and its crumbly moon-colored lotus paste.

It did seem like love had bloomed then, he thinks sometimes, but he is not so sure now. What is certain is that *she* bloomed. She filled out, developed breasts that grew to the size of the *tang bao zi*, the bun for which the tea house was famous.

More dumpling than bread, *tang bao zi* suspended mouth-searing broth in a nearly paper thin, immaculately crafted envelope of dough, so delicate that each bun came in its own bamboo basket, with a straw sticking out of its nipple-shaped top. There was no way he could steal this bun; and even if he could, the soup would leak out long before he got home, this he knew. Many were the nights he'd gazed enviously at the customers sucking the soup through their straws. He would dream of *tang bao zi* on those evenings, his head nestled on her bosom.

He began to demand love after every shared meal, and she complied, often in good humor. In between sex, she studied her lessons—he supposes this is what she must have done—for eventually, she graduated from city college, passed the Pharmacy board exam. The city college hung a banner outside the gate with her name and photo as though she were a local celebrity. His role in her success—this was not lost upon him: He considered this his greatest achievement—for a long time ago, he himself had been frustrated by his inability to graduate from high school, a failure that haunted him daily.

Perhaps this is why, in spite of the care with which they had phrased their love in the terms of a fair exchange, he did not immediately understand when he came home one morning and found her nowhere—when she did not return the next morning, or the morning after that. And even after he'd finally found the note she had carefully wedged into a crack in the floor, underneath the door ("We both knew this would end. Thanks for everything."), even after he'd admitted to himself that she was right, he was shocked by the suddenness of her departure, and his own irrational conviction that it was she, in the end, who had somehow broken their agreement, had revealed some shortsighted folly, such ingratitude.

Now she works at the pharmacy, a short distance from the tea house. Out of habit he checks on her every morning, hands her a bun or two in a plastic bag. One does what one can with what he is given.

If he is early enough, he helps her lift the aluminum security gate, then watches as she checks the inventory and rearranges the display. They say nothing to each other. When he is late he listens to her banter with the customers, she, competent and smart in her white uniform, her blouse, tight against her chest. On these mornings, he doesn't stay very long. He turns away when he feels a familiar tightening in his own chest, a lump in his throat.

HE FINDS IT in the back alley, mewling piteously in the shadows. He stops, in the early morning drizzle, to look at it closely: A tiny kitten, possibly no more than a week old, crouched on all fours, shivering; its white fur matted with mud, its eyes still shut. From the corner of his eye, he sees a dark shadow scamper past. He imagines bloody remains in the alley; this makes him feel sick. He puts the kitten in his jacket's breast pocket, where, for a few moments, it hisses and squirms, and then settles, soothed no doubt by the sound of his heartbeat. He begins walking again.

She is already assisting a few customers when he arrives. He places the bag of buns on the counter and waits for her acknowledgment, a nod—for only then would he leave.

Suddenly he yelps—sharp scratches sting his breast. He pulls out the kitten, which has begun to yowl, the muddy fur on its neck pinched between his thumb and forefinger. He drops it on the counter then looks inside his shirt to check for injuries.

"Take that away!" the pharmacist's assistant hisses, without looking at him. The customers stare at him, and then at the kitten curling its tiny body into a muddy mound on the counter.

"He works at The Garden of the Coming Happiness," one of the customers says to her companion, "Brings her *siu bao* every morning."

"And what is that," the gentleman says, nodding toward the kitten, "the new dimsum on the menu?" They titter.

The guard scoops up the kitten into his palm, leaving muddy streaks on the counter.

"Found it this morning," he whispers, thrusting the kitten towards his old sweetheart.

"I said take it away. Can't have dirt around here." She takes out a rag and wipes the mud off the counter.

He watches her rub the spot on the counter vigorously, considers what to say next.

"What to feed it?"

"Why not catch some mice?" says the gossipy customer, narrowing her eyes.

"Or bring home some of those buns from the tea house," her companion says, in a tone that is neither helpful nor sincere. The crowd by the counter giggles.

And perhaps, she begins to pity him then (had he not been always gentle with her, always generous with the little he had?) for she finally turns, looks at him, and says, with a sigh:

"Perhaps milk?"

"Perfect."

"But it will cost you."

He shrugs.

She hands him a can of infant formula.

"One part powder for every three parts water."

He gives her his week's wages—all that she asks—the price of milk surprises him somewhat. He drops the kitten into his pocket, looks at her hopefully. But she turns away, begins to assist other customers.

He decides to head home.

HIS ROOM HAS never seemed as empty and as sad. Beyond the open door, the single bed and its rumpled sheet by the makeshift wooden bench. The single shelf beneath the narrow clerestory window, the only ventilation in the tiny room. The single lightbulb hanging from the ceiling. The sad table with the lonely thermos, the chipped cup and saucer set, the orphan spoon. The sorry box of clothes underneath. Where to put the kitten? He wonders.

He shuts the window and sets it on his bed. He wets a sheet of newspaper with the water from his thermos and wipes it down. Underneath the mud, he finds tiny pink nubs on its chest—it is female. He watches as it—she—dries her damp fur by kneading her body against the bed sheet. He makes some milk and pours a little into the saucer. He sets the dish on the bed, by the kitten. It sniffs the milk, and rejects it. He presses her head down gently with his forefinger. The kitten sneezes into the milk. He picks her up by the neck. She opens her mouth, toothless still, as though ready to suckle.

And then suddenly—it happens so fast—the kitten curls into a ball and its hind legs frantically claw through the air. They reach beyond its tiny head, scratch the thumb and forefinger holding the patch of skin on the kitten's neck. A claw digs painfully into the tip of his thumb, making him release his grip. But the claw, now firmly embedded, rips through the thumb, dragging with it a tiny strip of flesh. The kitten falls to the floor, yowling. His thumb begins to bleed.

The kitten picks herself up. Trembling, she sniffs her way toward the bleeding hand and burrows her tiny head into his palm. She licks the blood off his thumb and with her tongue begins to make excited, clicking noises. She begins to suck, weakly at first. But soon, she is taking long deep draughts. He watches, mesmerized, as she feasts. She sucks on his thumb for hours; her appetite is insatiable. When he allows himself to finally drift off, his last sensation is of the kitten rubbing her rough tongue on the knuckle of his thumb, as though in gratitude.

HE AWAKENS IN the early evening. He hears the soft clicking of her tongue, and feels her rub her behind against the back of his hand. A damp warmth trickles onto his skin. He shakes her off and wipes his hand on the bed cover. He checks the time and finds he's already two hours late for his shift. He feels dizzy, and tired beyond belief. He decides to take the rest of the night off.

The kitten saunters onto his chest, twice as big as she was when he found her. That doesn't seem right, he says to himself. And so he sits up to examine the kitten.

He finds that her eyes have opened, but they remain unseeing—black-blue pupils staring blankly beyond. She rubs her face against his hand and sniffs out the wound on his thumb. It is still fresh and bleeding slightly. He snatches his hand, and stands up to make some milk.

When he takes a sip, the kitten begins to purr. He pours a little milk into the saucer and sets it on the bench. The kitten jumps from bed to bench, but refuses to lick the milk on the saucer. He dips his forefinger into the milk and brings it to her mouth. She runs her tongue over the milk-stained finger, and then latches on to it. But the latch turns into a bite—had the kitten grown teeth overnight? He tries shaking it off his hand, but the kitten is stronger, he fails this time. With a new wound to suckle, she is perfectly content. He is less certain about his feelings. He watches the kitten and tries to think about what she is doing—what he is allowing her to do.

But making sense is not his strong suit: He decides to make the best of things instead. With his free hand, he lifts the cup of milk to his lips. After all, there are many ways one can be useful, obtain affection. After all, one does what one can, with what he is given.

WHEN HE COMES to, it is as if an axe had cracked open his skull.

The kitten is beside him, asleep, curled into a ball, the size, he thinks, of a small melon, or a breast. Or a *tang bao zi*, he says to himself bitterly.

He examines his hand, now with two fresh wounds. The wound on the forefinger scares him a little—an inch of flesh appears to have been bitten off, or chewed through. But because he feels no pain other than the throbbing in his temples—his hand is completely numb—he does not believe the wounds pose any real danger. He wraps his hand in a clean shirt and staggers to work.

From the street, he can tell it is business as usual at the tea house. The crowd is thick, each slurping member oblivious to the burping other.

He enters the alley and then the steam-filled kitchen, is assaulted by the thick smell of processed pork and acrid anise. The cloying plum and nutty sesame; the burnt sugar and honey soy; the pungent vinegar and smoky tea—they all make him heady with desire. On the dimsum cart, he espies a *tang bao zi*, newly steamed, sweating inside its bamboo basket. He becomes aware of a terrible ache in the pit of his stomach, a sourness in his mouth. He reaches for the *tang bao zi* with his uninjured hand, and knocks down the straw, which rips off the flesh of the damp white mound. The scalding broth squirts through the broken dough, lands on the back of his hand. He screams. Someone wrestles him down, pours ice water. Out of nowhere appears the chef, immaculate in his white uniform. A slap on the face, a kick in the gut. Strong arms drag him out the kitchen and into the alley.

He looks up and sees a man in uniform—his uniform, it was his name embroidered above the left breast pocket, wasn't it?—the face of a stranger.

"You've never been any trouble before," the usurper says. The click of a lighter, the smell of cheap cigarette blown his way. "Same post. Five unremarkable years." The man in his uniform takes a long drag. "That's what they said at the agency."

"The agency?"

"The agency sent me. You'd been gone a week. Nobody knew what had happened to you—"

"A week—?"

"You know how it is, *kaibigan*, you and I do."

"That's impossible! I—"

But what to tell him? That he'd spent a week feeding a kitten? Having a kitten feed on him? He tries to make sense of things but there is the pulsing weight in his head, the hole boring into the pit of his stomach, the wind like nails on his raw skin.

He shakes off the shirt in which he'd wrapped the other hand, the one on which the kitten had suckled. There they still are, two gaping wounds, one on the thumb, the other on the forefinger. The kitten, the kitten. Its bloody remains in the alley. He'd left it in the alley, and now this. Two gaping wounds in the bloody alley. The kitten in the alley. No, the kitten at home. Strength in his aching legs. Strength to stand, scamper past the uniform and down the alley.

MUDDY AND SHIVERING, he pushes himself into his room. He is startled by the odors of the tea house. And then the presence of a stranger, standing in the shadows.

"It will be better for you if you do not turn on the light," she says in a low, silky voice. "Come nearer. I smell your despair."

But he does not move, so it is she who comes closer—a platinum blonde with blank, dark blue eyes and skin white as milk. She is wearing a white pelt coat and the smell of plum and sesame; sugar and soy; barbecued pork; black vinegar.

"Fear," she sniffs, her odor overpowering, swirling round him. "But you have no need to fear me." She licks his earlobe tentatively, and walks back into the shadows.

"I want you to come to me."

And so he does. He rubs his wet cheek on the white pelt coat. It is warm, dry, fragrant with a hundred remembered odors from the tea house—beansprouts and pickles; black sesame and sweet bean; lotus paste and crab roe.

The stranger runs her fingers in his damp hair, digs her nails, claw-like, into his scalp. He moves in to kiss her. As he draws near, he feels the soft furry down of her face. She pushes his head down toward her chest, where, beneath the fur coat, he finds the skin smooth and milky, and a breast, soft and firm like a warm steamed bun. His mouth makes its way toward the nipple and is amply rewarded; his numb, injured hands find other breasts to fondle; his feet find their own warmth; his toes latch on to the softness elsewhere. There is plenty of her to go around.

He dreams he is dining at The Garden of the Coming Happiness. He is served basket after basket of *tang bao zi*. He kisses each immaculate curve then tears the delicate skin with his teeth. His tongue is efficient, lapping up quickly the ambrosia within. In his dream, the dimsum service is endless.

Hours later, fully sated, he drops from her chest, scampers out the door, and runs on all fours, away into the morning.

GABRIELA LEE *has an MA in Literary Studies from the National University of the Philippines, and a BA in Creative Writing from the University of the Philippines (Diliman). She has been published for her poetry and fiction in English in the Philippines and abroad. She was a fellow for poetry in English at the UP, Iligan, and Dumaguete National Writers Workshops. She can be found at http://about.me/gabrielalee*

# August Moon

## Gabriela Lee

I WOKE UP with a crick in my neck, my head bent at an awkward angle. Bright globes of light wavered at the periphery of my vision. I straightened up from my seat and rubbed the sleep from my eyes.

The room was small and smelled of stale candle wax and incense. The walls were decorated with sconces and images of saints. There were five wooden pews on either side, and an aisle with a threadbare red carpet running down the middle. Flowers bloomed at every corner—funeral wreaths of lilies and ferns and baby's-breath. Candles flickered at the far end of the room. I felt like I had stepped into a place that was forgotten in time.

Slowly, I stood up from my seat, a white plastic chair that had been shoved into the corner of the room near the door. I don't remember how I got here, or where here was, but I could feel a little tug in my chest, as though someone had tied an invisible string around it and was pulling me towards them. I stepped closer, my heels digging into the rug. The aisle seemed to go on forever, and then then I was there.

A lacquered wooden coffin was laid out in front of me, the dark wood reflecting back the glimmer of candlelight. The lid was closed, but at the head of the casket there was a large gilt frame with a picture of a man—slanted eyes, straight black hair swept off his forehead, skin the color of parchment. He wore a brown collared shirt and smiled with his lips, not with his eyes. Beside the frame was a small table, where a guestbook was flipped open. The lines carried names, unfamiliar names in unfamiliar scrawls. Anita Lim, one name read gracefully. Jason Lim. Caleb Lim. Cat Lim. There were a lot of Lims in the book. Perhaps the family name?

Beside the guestbook, there was a narrow vase filled with joss sticks, the smoke trickling from the blackened tips. A fat white candle sat beside it. Beside the candle was a stack of what seemed to be paper money.

There was a rustling beside me, and I turned to excuse myself. I probably wasn't supposed to be here. A slight panic started to build in my chest. How did I even get here in the first place? I couldn't even remember—

The lady to my right stood in front of the photograph. She was perhaps old enough to be the mother of the man in the photo. She was dressed in a loose cotton blouse, like the ones you see people wear on safari, and black pants. Her hair was pulled up in a bun, and I could see that her eyes were red-rimmed, the tears refusing to fall. Strands of beads were wrapped around her fist—scarlet rosary beads, the color of dried blood.

I shifted away from her, seating myself on the nearest pew. There was something about this woman that I found fascinating. Each movement of hers was small, economical, precise. She wasn't wearing any jewelry except for a plain gold band around the fourth finger of her left hand. She stared at the display for a few minutes, her heart in her eyes, and then moved towards the small table.

She took one piece of the paper money left at the side and held its tip towards the unsteady flame. I watched as the paper shriveled and blackened and crumbled to ash, smoke curling upwards like strange alien writing, finally disappearing into the stale air-conditioned air. Then she turned around, her eyes gliding over me, and then walked away from the coffin.

Mommy. The word, unbidden, came to my lips. It struggled against the closed slit of my mouth, pummeling the soft flesh until I was forced to open it. Mommy.

The woman turned back once, her eyes watery with tears, like a pond shimmering with fresh-fallen rain. And then she was gone.

I don't remember having a mother. I don't even remember who I am! I blinked once, twice, trying to stem the rising wave of panic that was bubbling up my throat. Think, think. Think, dammit!

My hands scrabbled in my pockets for any sort of information. I came up with a handful of junk: a used tissue, some hair ties, and half-eaten packet of Juicy Fruit. There's also a torn movie ticket stub. It's for some stupid action film, but the date was printed on the flimsy piece of card. August 7, 2007. What a coincidence. The movie stub was from Greenbelt 5, which meant that I probably came from there. Good, now we're getting somewhere.

I stood up and sidled against the wall, trying not to draw attention to myself. There were still mourners scattered on the pews, seated in ones and twos and threes. Heads leaning against each, or nestled on shoulders, as though nobody in the room could hold their heads up high. I made my way towards the door and pushed it open.

Outside, the world was already dark. I stepped out on to a balcony that seemed to run down the length of the building, overlooking the nighttime street. The funeral parlor seemed to be on the second floor of a three-storey structure. A cement staircase with a wrought-iron railing twisted along one side of the balcony. Wooden benches lined one side, and a bunch of men were clustered together, clutching sweating bottles of San Miguel, and smoking. The heavy smell of Marlboro hung in the air, along with a faint undertone of days-old dogshit and diesel fumes.

Above the corrugated tin roofs and ramshackle tiles, past the tangle of electric and cable wires mounted on wooden poles, beyond this inexplicable moment of not knowing who I was and where I came from and what the fuck I was doing in a funeral home in the middle of nowhere, there was the moon, hung up in the sky like a milky opal on an invisible pendant. It loomed over me, bathing the tops of trees and the garbage spilling over the streets in an ethereal glow. A slight breeze ruffled the edge of my skirt, the curling tips of my hair. It was getting late. I needed to figure out how to get home. Well, no, first I needed to figure out where home was.

I approached the huddle of men at the corner of the balcony cautiously. Maybe one of them would recognize me? It was a long shot, if I was actually meant to even be here, but a long shot was better than no shot at all.

"—Clark still owes me a hundred pesos," said one of the men conversationally, taking a swig of his beer. "Gave him money last week for his whore so that she could take a cab going back to Mandaluyong"

"That girl wearing those short shorts?" asked another man. "Pare, she was hot. I'd do her in a minute."

"You'd only last a minute, Ted!"

The group roared with laughter. I shuffled towards the edge, keeping myself to the shadows. These people felt— odd, somehow. Strange yet familiar. I didn't know who they were, but they flitted around the edge of my memory, as if I should know them. But I didn't. I wanted to listen to what they were saying before I opened my mouth.

The first man was speaking again. He seemed to be the center of the group—everyone else surrounded him like moths drawn to a flame. He raised his almost-empty beer bottle in a toast. Five or six other bottles clinked against his. "To Clark, the best motherfucker in town. And when I say 'motherfucker', I mean—"

"Shhh, Chris, shhh. Tita's coming out."

The door swung open a second time and an elderly lady, leaning on a cane, peered from the edge of the door with rheumy eyes. "Are you all behaving yourselves?" she asked in a quavering voice.

"Yes, Tita," they all chorused, like a bunch of high school boys caught in the backyard, sneaking alcohol from the kitchen.

"Has anyone seen Des? I need my medicine from the car."

One of the younger men, not past boyhood, really, stood up and brushed invisible dirt off his button-down shirt. "I'll go down to the car, Ma. Maybe Des is sleeping inside."

"Thank you, Jason," she said, her body wavering as she tottered back inside.

Someone handed the boy a five hundred peso bill. "Get a case of San Mig as well."

"All by myself?"

"Sean, go with him."

The two shuffled off, disappearing down the stairs. I edged closer to the group, where the first man who spoke still held court. He looked so familiar: his dark hair swept back smoothly, high cheekbones, a smile that could cut through cold butter. I peered through the grimy window that looked into the room. Someone had started burning more of the paper money; the almost-invisible smoke seemed to writhe and take shape above the casket. It seemed to me that they looked like long fingers, spreading above the heads of the few mourners that were left in the room, reaching towards me...

I looked down at my own hands. They shimmered faintly in the cool light of the naked fluorescent bulbs that were strung along the eaves. My palms were translucent, allowing me to see the floor underneath, the skin cool like a passing wind. I blinked back tears.

I was dead. I knew it for a certainty.

The smoke filtered through the gaps between the windows, the thin space that separated the door frame and the wall, quickly wrapping me up in its grip. I could smell charred paper, carbon and, underneath it all, a lick of fire. Chris, I remembered. His name is Chris.

"Wonder if they found her body," he was saying to the group. "I'd want a shot at that bitch myself."

Someone interjected: "You know there's no proof that –"

"I don't care!" His voice carried down to the busy street below; a few passersby looked up, searching for the source of the sound. "Clark was nothing but decent to her, and I know, I know she killed him. Fucking cunt. She deserves everything that happened to her."

"Let's face it, Chris. Clark wasn't exactly blameless, you know."

"Fuck you. You don't know him. And what's a few girls, huh? Everyone does it. You've got every right to look for pussy when your wife refuses to fuck you, all right? He had every right." Chris' eyes were now red, his cheeks flushed, the scent of alcohol clinging to his lips like a lover's kiss.

I remembered him now. Chris Uy, financial broker, weekend basketball player, going through girlfriends the way some men went through bottles of beer. Come to think of it, he probably treated beer better. He drove a sleek car, all silver and leather and faux wood. He changed phones every two weeks, but was partial to his Blackberry. And he was—

He was—

Why can't I remember?

Images flashed in my head, quickly flipping from one moment to another as though someone was manning a hyperactive projector. There: white lace and silk, a flowing river of lilies of the valley being gripped by sweaty hands. Light streaming through stained glass windows. The tight, almost painful grasp of someone's hands on my shoulders. Bruises blossoming along my arm like sea anemones. Long woolen sleeves, a wedding ring choking the fourth finger of my left hand. Delicate cuts, healing into invisible white scars.

The moon hid behind a bank of passing clouds. The boys, Sean and Jason, had returned with a case of beer, amber bottles tucked into a battered plastic case. Condensation coated the glass, dripped down the floor. Another toast, another chime of celebration for the life that was lost. I wondered why I was haunting someone else's funeral—that's what they called it, right? A haunting.

I looked back at my hands. The tips of my fingers had disappeared, the nails all but gone. Wisps of imagined flesh trailed across the air, silver and faint. I was vanishing, even from my own sight, and I didn't even know who I was, or what I was doing here.

Well, I knew a bit more now. The woman in the room was familiar enough, and the men outside were faces I could match names to. And I knew where I came from, well, before I died. Still, there was a gap between watching a movie at Greenbelt and suddenly finding out that one was a ghost, and I wanted to bridge that gap as soon as possible.

I drifted back into the funeral room. The clock on the wall said that it was 2:10 in the morning. I wasn't sure how many days people had been mourning, but from the looks of it, this wasn't the first day. Walking down the aisle once more, I sat beside two older women, one of them the elderly lady with the cane that the men referred to as their aunt.

"Is there any news?" asked one of them, her elegant fingers folded on her lap.

"Anna says that the police had have just finished cataloging the crime scene. We'll probably know in a few days. Don't worry, Anita. I'm sure they'll find her."

Anita looked down at her hands, the nails lacquered scarlet. They stood out starkly against her all-white ensemble. "Do you think she's still alive?"

Tita shook her white head sadly. "Heaven forbid that girl is still alive."

"How can you say that?" Her tone was shocked.

"Can you imagine? The family will never forgive her. She'll be forced out with nothing more than the clothes on her back. Her name will be forgotten. No, it's better if she was dead. You can't blame the dead for the sins of the living."

"But Tita…" Anita's voice trailed off and she looked around, checking to see if anyone was listening. Her voice fell to an almost whisper. "Do you think the rumors are true, though? About Clark and—"

"Oh, they're true, all right."

I felt a shiver down my spine.

"I saw her once. The girl, I mean. They were in the mall—I was buying a present for Carlito, remember, his birthday was three months ago? He held her in a way he'd never held Adele. She was very small, very pale. Looked like a doll, all big eyes and red lips. I can see why he was…enamored of her." Tita licked her lips, her eyes shining. "My husband had a querida once, when we were young. I told him to leave her or he'd never see Jason again."

"Too bad they didn't have children," said Anita. "Maybe Adele could have used that as leverage."

"No." Tita shook her head. "He would have gladly left Adele for this woman, I'm sure of it."

"Sad. It's always sad."

My heart sank like a stone in my chest. The poor woman. Abandoned, left on her own. Somehow, the pieces were all swirling in my head, puzzle bits attempting to fit their uneven edges together to form a picture. The smell of smoke encircled me, made me feel lightheaded.

Hands. Stained hands. Standing in the kitchen, the bright white lights harsh and unforgiving. A twisted wrist, a pleading voice. What was happening? I felt like I was watching a horror movie in jump cuts, the camera wobbling in fear. The scent of iron and prayer in the air. Tiles, slick and dark. The echo of a scream staining the walls of the room.

I leaned back against the wooden pew, my breath coming in short, sharp gasps. Was that how Clark Lim died? Was that how—wait, no, that was a woman on the floor, her flesh in ribbons, her blood on the tiles. Her eyes were staring at the ceiling, the gaze blank.

"Her mother wants to bury her in the family plot," said Anita, returning me back to their conversation. "Of course, she still blames Papa for all of this."

"Your father has very traditional views, Anita. You know that. You, of all people, know that." The older woman's voice was gentle.

"Yes, but Harv's a good man. He'd...he'd never do what Clark did. And I can't believe I'm saying this, but Clark deserves this. I saw Adele a few weeks after their wedding, when she visited for lunch. She looked like someone had used her face as a punching bag." Anita's voice trembled. "I wanted to take her to the doctor, but she said she just fell down the stairs."

"Why didn't you tell us?"

"Her father was happy, and so was Papa. After all, they would never have gotten a better business deal than that. And it was a good match, you know? We know Adele's family, and Clark had been nursing that crush on her since grade school. She's just shy, he said. Never had a boyfriend before. You know how they talk. Plus Papa's like, coming from some medieval fantasy film and we 'have to preserve the purity of the blood line.' I mean, at least I knew Harv from school and we knew the same people, had common friends. But Adele and Clark barely spoke to each other, you know what I mean? She probably had no idea what she was getting herself into. I mean, I knew Clark had a violent streak, but nothing like this."

Both women fell silent, and I slipped out of the pew and started walking towards the front of the room. Even without looking, I knew that my feet had disappeared, that I was simply floating, moving my legs with muscle memory. I don't know how I remained upright, how I moved, except that my mind commanded it and my body obeyed. Maybe this is why ghosts seem so incomplete, so transitory. The more they remember their past, the faster their present fades, like the way sunlight dispels fog.

I stood in front of the photograph on display, searching the easy smile for a clue to his betrayal. It was simple, really—nobody gets what they wanted. And there was nothing anyone could do about it. It was like trapping an ant inside a honey maze, a bird inside a gilded cage. No matter how beautiful the prison is, it's still a prison. Perhaps that was how Adele felt, thrust into a situation she barely had any control over. Clark's smile was open, bright. Perhaps that was how he smiled at her, at first, before any of this had happened. And now, well. Now it was just too late.

A knot of people—teenage girls, young cousins perhaps, approached the coffin to pay their respects. I stepped aside, even though I knew they couldn't see me. I wondered how bad the injuries were that even the mortician was unable to stitch him back up. A knife could fillet even the strongest of men, if used right. They moved through the steps, punctuating the ritual with the burning of the paper money.

The flame touched the delicate surface of the paper, heat causing the sheet to curl, blacken, ash drifting downwards. The scent of it assaulted my nose, causing my head to hurt. Again, and again, and again, the acrid smell hit me, filling my lungs with smoke. I coughed, my eyes watering. This was too much—

And then, and then, and then I remembered.

My husband was not a kind man, nor was he a good man. He was unbound by tradition in the way that I was bound by it. A good wife did not complain, did not cry, did not say that the world was unfair. A good wife forgave and forgot. Except, I think, some things did not deserve forgiveness, or forgetfulness.

I already knew he was sleeping around. I knew that, as much as I knew that he enjoyed hurting me. What I didn't know was that he was in love. He said as much as we drove back into the house after the movie. I remember the night was dark, the stars obscured by pollution and city lights. Only the moon hung high enough to still shine. We stepped into the kitchen. He dropped his keys into the bowl by the door. I felt something inside me snap, like a rubber band stretched too thin, too far apart. I remember grabbing the knife from the block, waving the blade in his face. The fear in his eyes. I remember the pain in my shoulder from where he'd hit me the last time, radiating down my arm.

More paper, more flames, candle wax dripping down in white globes to harden around the base of the candle. Everything was gray-wisped, painted behind smoke and mirrors. The images were moving faster, faster, flicking through my mind like a high-speed camera. They kept on burning paper, watching in fascination as the delicate fibers twisted from one form to another, solid and liquid and gas.

I remember the woman knocking on the door, surprised that I was home. I tucked the knife behind my back, pulling on my sleeves to cover the stains. I remember asking her, plain and pleasant, to follow me to the kitchen, that my husband was waiting for her. I could see the fear in her eyes, the apology. She wanted to say that she was sorry. I had no use for her apologies. I remember that she smelled of nervous sweat and Chanel No. 5. I remember carving her up like a spring chicken while she screamed.

I could still hear her screams.

Perhaps this was my punishment. But is it really punishment, knowing that they deserved it? I was a good wife. I did everything he asked me to do, and more.

I am a good wife.

I looked down at my body, the clothing blood-spattered, my arms stained with the shadow of blood. My body was already fading, going up like candle smoke. I knew in two days, the police would find my body hidden behind the azaleas, my wrists gaping open like twin mouths. The grass would be dark with my own death. I wondered if my eyes would be open or closed. I hoped they'd be open. I wanted to see the moon.

PAOLO CHIKIAMCO *has placed in the Palanca Awards, and his short stories have been published in the* Digest of Philippine Genre Stories, The Best of Philippine Speculative Fiction 2009, *and the* Philippine Speculative Fiction *series. He is the writer of several comic books, including* High Society, *a steampunk alternative history. He is the editor of* Ruin and Resolve, *the* Usok *webzine, and most recently,* Alternative Alamat. *He is also a fantasy fiction slush reader for* Lightspeed *Magazine. Rocket Kapre, his publishing imprint and blog dedicated to publishing and promoting Speculative Fiction by Filipino authors, can be found at http://rocketkapre.com/*

# The Captain's Nephew

## Paolo Chikiamco

BACOOR. 1897.

"GET DOWN!"

The captain pulled his nephew back into the trench just as a barrage of gunfire from the Spanish soldiers perforated the air. The young Chinese man glared at his uncle with barely suppressed fury.

"What did you do that for?"

An older Katipunero rapped the captain's nephew soundly on his *salakot*. "Your uncle saved your life. Show some gratitude!"

But the young man would not be placated. "I had a shot!"

"So did they," said the captain, in a dry tone of voice. "What's the point of these defenses if you refuse to use them?"

"We shouldn't be hiding in the first place. We should charge forward, guns blazing and—"

"—cause the rest of our men to leave cover and get shot full of bullets?" The captain's voice turned hard. "I will not throw away lives. Caution before glory, understand?"

The captain's nephew grit his teeth, but then nodded. He opened his mouth to say more when another young Katipunero rolled into the trench, breathing hard. By chance or by design, he'd made it to their position while the Spanish were reloading their guns. The Governor-General's forces across the bridge had yet to stagger their fire, a small blessing which the captain was happy to take.

"General Evangelista's position is under heavy assault," the new arrival gasped. "General Aguinaldo commands that you give assistance."

The captain swore. He looked at his small contingent of men, then set his jaw. "On my count, we advance."

His nephew was already hefting his rifle. "What happened to caution?"

"It's a leader's prerogative to endanger his men," said the captain. "Just remember that it's not one to be used without good reason."

The Katipuneros fired a few cautious shots from the cover of the trench, enough to bait an answering barrage from the Spanish. When the sound of gunfire ceased, the captain gave the signal to move. The captain went first. It was his way.

That's why the first indication they had of the enemy's change of tactics was when Captain Paua tumbled back into the trench, echoes of the salvo that felled him still ringing in the air.

## BATANGAS. 1896.

THE FOREST THAT covered the slopes of Mount Pico de Loro was thick with dense underbrush and slim, swaying trees whose trunks formed a lattice of rough bark and sharp edges. The trunks were almost invisible beneath the shelter of the forest canopy, deeper lines of black obstructing stray beams of moonlight and frustrating the efforts of one Chinese man. Jose Ignacio Paua swung his bolo once more at a particularly stubborn patch of bamboo, then stopped to wipe his brow. Not for the first time that night, the Katipunero mused that the forest was a decidedly unwelcoming place. This was not, however, an observation that deterred him. Paua was a man accustomed to walking where he was not wanted, in places where he was in danger from far worse than an errant branch.

Of course, there was always the chance that something more sinister than a tree was lurking on this mountain. In fact, that was what Paua was counting on.

After a good three hours of stumbling and hacking his way up the mountainside, Paua eventually emerged onto a flat outcropping within sight of the beak-shaped summit which gave the mountain its name. This high above sea level, the night breeze was cold enough to make Paua shiver, and strong enough to make his queue—his long, braided ponytail—dance. For a moment, the Katipunero looked to the east, and fancied he could see all the way to Imus, and the scowling visage of Pantaleon Garcia.

"This is a fool's errand," Pantaleon had told him. "You're chasing after tuba-fueled nightmares, or some oddly shaped shadow."

"Shadows don't smoke cigars," Paua had replied as he mounted his horse. "I'll be in the area anyway for recruitment. No harm in taking a look."

"Of course not. Not for you. Not when there's an adventure to be had."

That was partly true. At twenty-four years old, Paua still had much of the restless energy which had driven him, six years ago, to leave China for the Philippines. But it was more than that. Paua moved to the very edge of the outcropping and took in the sight of his adopted home. To the south, the mountains of Batangas rose above the rolling green countryside; to the north the island of Bataan was just visible over the water. Pantaleon was his friend, but there was no way that anyone who had lived for forty years in this country could fully understand Paua's hunger to explore it.

It was only when Paua reluctantly tore himself away from the view that he realized that he was not alone. A man in dark red clothes leaned against one of the taller trees, a somewhat twisted looking plant with round, low-hanging leaves. The overhanging branches kept most of the man's face in shadow, but Paua could see enough to identify him as Chinese.

"Are you lost, neighbor?" said the man in red. "You're a long way from home."

When Paua made no reply, the other man moved out of the shade of the tree. As the man moved closer, Paua scrutinized his face carefully under the moonlight.

"I could show you the way back down the mountain," said the man in red. His face was round and ruddy, his smile open and guileless. "I'm on my way back down myself."

"Oh, I remember you now," said Paua in Hokkien. "That's clever."

The man in red stopped, his expression darkening. "I'm sorry, I did not quite hear you."

"I was commending you on your ingenuity," Paua said, shifting back to Tagalog. "I figured it would be difficult to try your usual trick, given that none of my relations would be anywhere near Cavite, let alone this mountain. Taking the face of an almost forgotten cousin and assuming the role of a helpful stranger...that was unexpected."

The man in red drew a large cigar from his pocket, and placed it between his lips. The tip of the cigar flared, and in that instant the man vanished. In his stead hulked a gangly figure that easily topped seven feet, its arms so long that one hairy hand was at the level of its knobby knees. The other hand still held the cigar, and against the backdrop of the night sky, the dull red light cast the figure's equine head into relief.

"A hunter." The Tikbalang's sigh sounded like a horse's nicker. "Hunters make for such poor sport. As you will, then. Shall it be salt first? One of your Christian beads? Or simply the business end of your blade?"

"What? No, no." Paua slowly returned the bolo to the sheath which hung from his waist. "I'm not here to hurt you."

The Tikbalang whinnied, and gave its head a shake, its long mane trailing behind like a coarse and tangled pennant. "Let us presume for a moment that your intentions have any bearing on what actually happens this night. Why are you here then, *banyaga*?"

Paua felt a rush of anger, but fought it down. One did not begin a courtship with threats and bombast. Instead Paua forced a smile and said: "I'm here to recruit you."

For the next twenty minutes, the young man spoke passionately about the Katipunan and the Revolution, the righteousness of their mission and the depredations of the Spanish. It was a spiel he'd given many times before, but never to so difficult an audience. Even those unwilling to take up arms against "Mother Spain" would at least admit to the existence of rumors of abuse and injustice. The Tikbalang, however, lacked both knowledge and sympathy.

"Such hubris, to strive to grasp what one cannot hold. Can you eat a 'cause'? Mate with 'liberty'? Fill your lungs with 'equality'?" The Tikbalang snorted and stomped a hoof against the dirt. "It is folly, human folly, and you are welcome to it. As for me, I have the scent of the sea, the touch of the night, and the shape of the land. I am content."

Paua's hand tightened on the hilt of his sword. He could feel the heat rising in his chest, emanating from the memory of bloody hands and bowed heads, burnt homes and tear-streaked faces. Faces he knew. Faces he could name.

"You are *content*," Paua bit out the last word as a curse. "You look down from your mountain and you think you know the land? You know smoke and shadow and dim, distant lights."

"You accuse me of ignorance?" The Tikbalang flared its nostrils, and surged forward. For a frightening moment

Paua thought it was going to charge. Instead it nickered once more, its expression—as best as Paua could tell—amused. "I had run the length and breadth of these islands a dozen times over before your Spaniards first set out to conquer. You, on the other hand, still smell of *longan*, tea leaves, and foreign hills. And you accuse me of ignorance?"

Paua stared up at the towering creature, not five feet from him, and weighed his options. After a moment, he lowered his gaze and looked away, mumbling something under his breath.

"What was that, *banyaga*?" The Tikbalang's voice was filled with glee, for such creatures love nothing more than to confuse and confound the mortal mind. It leaned in close to the Katipunero, its teeth shockingly white in the darkness. "I did not quite hear you."

"I said that there are indeed many things I do not know," said Paua. "But I do know that you shouldn't be standing so close."

With a sweep of his arm, Paua pulled three hairs from the Tikbalang's mane. The creature reared to its full height, letting out a roar that no horse could ever have made, but Paua had already leaped on to the back of the Tikbalang, both arms locked around its neck.

The creature plunged through the dense forest, rough branches and razor-thin leaves leaving Paua's shirt a tattered mess that just barely clung to his back, which itself was crisscrossed by innumerable lacerations, both deep and shallow. Still, Paua clung on. The stories that Paua had heard from the old folk prepared him for the Tikbalang's sudden surge.

The plunge off the side of the mountain, however, was another story.

Paua's screams were whipped away by the wind, then left behind completely as the Tikbalang banked sharply downward, toward the sea. The Katipunero had just enough time to register the fact that the Tikbalang was in complete control of its descent before he and the creature plunged into the cold waters off the coast of Batangas. The salt water stitched lines of pain across his skin, and Paua's lungs were burning before the Tikbalang once more launched itself into the open air. Still, Paua clung on.

The Tikbalang shed water as it rose into the air, picking up even more speed the higher it climbed. By the time Paua had coughed up the sea from his lungs, they were already beyond the peak of Mount Pico de Loro. As the air thinned around him, a strange thing happened. The young man's senses seemed to sharpen, and the night sky took on a peculiar clarity, of the sort possessed by the most vivid of dreams. Paua was filled with a sudden certainty that if he only released his grip on the Tikbalang, he would float up to the moon, and hold the stars in his hands. For a moment the Katipunero's hands slackened—but just for a moment.

Paua clung on.

After an unknowable span of time, the Tikbalang's hooves touched the ground once more, and Paua realized that they were back atop the very same outcropping where he had first laid eyes on the creature. The Tikbalang went down on one knee and remained in that position even after Paua slid off its back, the three precious hairs wrapped around his forefinger.

Paua circled slowly around the creature, hearing once more in his mind the legends that surrounded it, reevaluating what he had believed was plausible. The young man had heard the stories of the old Katipuneros at Imus, and again at Ternate, but surely reason would dictate that not everything could be true. Yet after such a ride, how much stock could be placed in reason?

As Paua finished his circuit, the Tikbalang raised its head and fixed the Katipunero with a steady gaze. Paua was startled at how human the Tikbalang's eyes were, visible whites surrounding the brown iris. There was pride in that gaze, and defiance—but underlying every other emotion was fear. A familiar fear, one that raised the hackles on the back of Paua's neck.

The Tikbalang spoke leadenly, as if its jaw was being forcibly manipulated. "What...would you have of me, Master?"

## BACOOR. 1897.

THE CAPTAIN'S NEPHEW moved with uncanny swiftness, catching his uncle in mid-fall and laying Paua down gently on the freshly turned soil. "Get me a doctor," he said, and while he did not shout, his voice rang in the ears of his fellow Katipuneros, and even those who outranked him would have rushed to obey, had the captain not spoken.

"Forward...next trench..." Paua hissed. He was bleeding profusely from multiple bullet wounds on his left chest. "Help Evangelista."

"No!" said the captain's nephew, and this time he did shout. "You need help."

"My needs...come last," replied the captain. He gripped his nephew by the wrist. "Stay here. The rest of you—move. That's an order."

The captain propped himself up on his elbows, and took slow, measured breaths until the rest of his men had gone. As the battle was joined, he met the eyes of his nephew, as familiar as his own.

"I can't die. Not yet. Not here." Paua coughed, and his nephew steadied him. "You know what you have to do."

## IMUS. 1896.

"YOU LET IT go?"

Pantaleon Garcia wore an expression caught halfway between skepticism and amusement. The old soldier tugged on the wide brim of his hat and shook his head. "Of course you did. If I didn't know you better, I'd say that you're making an excuse for returning empty handed."

"Not immediately. I just wanted an opportunity to really make my case." Paua took a sip of water from his mug, and let the fatigue from the day's exertions radiate from him in waves. Before he had gone on his last recruitment swing, he'd received word that the Magdalo commanders had agreed to his proposal to erect an ammunition and weapons factory in Imus. While he'd been on the mountain, Pantaleon had found a secluded clearing suitable for the site. They had gathered their small group of volunteers—many of whom were Chinese blacksmiths, like Paua himself—and begun construction that morning. Now the two senior Katipuneros were catching their breath atop a felled log, and contemplating how much work there was yet to be done.

"Don't look so disappointed, Pantaleon. It's not as if you believed the stories anyway."

"You've a history of surprising folk, my boy. Why stop now?" Pantaleon ran a finger across his moustache, then scowled at the moisture that had accumulated on it. "Still, reason aside, I'd be hard pressed to complain if we had a magical beast bound to obey our every command. Think of the treasures they have in the legends, or that magical stone... How it would stick in the craw of Bonifacio and his cohort if we had an army of invincible soldiers. God, wouldn't that be a sight, eh?"

"I should check if the men need any help moving the *lantakas*." Paua drained his mug, and then stood up. He kept his expression blank.

"You go on ahead," Pantaleon said, swallowing a groan. "Manual labor is a young man's affair."

To be honest, Paua didn't yet feel up to hauling the large canons to and fro—but he needed to put some space between himself and his friend. He owed much to the patronage of the old soldier, but there were times that he felt

Pantaleon forgot who the enemy was, or what they were fighting for.

Before Paua could reach the *lantakas*, however, he was intercepted by one of their perimeter watchmen.

"Sir," the watchman said, inclining his head toward Paua. "There's a young man looking for you. He says he's your nephew?"

Paua hesitated only a moment before replying. "Yes, of course. Where is he?"

The watchman led him to the very edge of the clearing, where another Katipunero kept a watchful eye on a young Chinese man, his hands bound by a rough hemp rope.

"We didn't want to take any chances," began the watchman, but Paua waved the explanation away.

"You did well. It was my fault that I neglected to inform you in advance." He looked at the young man, and the family resemblance was both uncanny and unnerving. "It's just that I wasn't sure he was coming."

The two watchmen untied the young man, who acknowledged their apologies with a polite nod, and then took their leave. After a moment, Paua began to walk, keeping to the edge of the clearing. The younger man paced him.

"Are you really walking around wearing my face?"

"A good guess," answered the Tikbalang. "It was your face, six years ago, or at least this is how it appears in your memory."

Paua didn't recall ever wearing such a delighted grin on his face, but then he remembered how much Tikbalangs were said to enjoy mischief. "I hope that's not how you looked when you went to Manila. There are people in the Parian who remember what I looked like at eighteen."

The Tikbalang's brow furrowed. "The Walled City. It is a cesspit."

Paua nodded, but kept silent. The Tikbalang had an expression that he'd seen often, that mixture of disbelief, disgust, and rage that came from the blinders being lifted. The Tikbalang told him of the things it had seen, in just two days of circulating amongst the people of Manila, both inside the walls and amongst the Chinese in the Parian. It told him how, as a Chinese man, it had been beaten for being within Manila during the *siesta* hours; how, as a Spaniard, a mother had offered herself if it would intercede with the guardia civil on her son's behalf; how, as a Filipino, it had fled after mistakenly assuming the form of a boy's dead mother.

"We can take the form that the human most expects to see," the Tikbalang explained. "The boy did not know she was dead, but his father..." It paused, and Paua watched as the face of his younger self was overtaken by staggering incomprehension. "What creature could take joy from that?"

The pair walked silently for a while. Paua waited for the Tikbalang to compose itself before asking, "I take it you have an answer to my invitation now?"

The Tikbalang stopped, forcing Paua to do the same. "It is forbidden for my people to interfere in the affairs of men. If I join your revolution, it must be as one of you."

"I understand."

"Many of the stories told about my kind are false. I have no treasure, no magic stone—those belong to other creatures, with less regard for man than me and mine."

"I understand."

"Then help *me* understand." The Tikbalang stepped closer to Paua, its nostrils flaring in a horse-like manner, its eyes—Paua's eyes—inches from his face. "If your need was so urgent, your cause so great—why did you set me free?"

Paua did not answer immediately. Instead, his right hand went to the queue at the back of his head. "In China, this braid represented loyalty to our foreign masters. When I first arrived in Manila, I thought I could finally cut it off. But there were masters here too. There are masters everywhere, it seems."

The Katipunero looked out at the construction site, where men and women, pale skinned and brown, labored to contribute in some small way to a greater dream. "I learned that oppression is not something you run from." Paua let his hand fall, and shook his head. "It's certainly not something you do to others."

A familiar voice shouted Paua's name, and Pantaleon made his way to the pair. "There you are," said the older Katipunero. "And here I thought you were already hard at work. Setting up this factory could take longer than expected."

"With respect, sir," the Tikbalang answered, before Paua could reply, "I think it will be ready by tomorrow."

Pantaelon squinted at the creature, his brow furrowing as he took in its resemblance to Paua. "Who's this? A new recruit?"

"Yes sir," the Tikbalang said, its voice giddy, its entire manner now that of an earnest youth. "Tiktik Ma, at your service."

"Good to meet you, Mr. Ma," Pantaleon said. He put an arm around the new recruit and steered him toward the canons. "Now, if those young arms can back up your bold prediction, I foresee a bright future for you!"

Later, witnesses will describe how Captain Paua shrugged off injuries that should have killed him, to lead his men across the Zapote Bridge. Some will whisper that Paua was hit but not injured, that he had an amulet that made him immune to bullets or blades. No, others will counter, it was a magic stone, a gift from a Tikbalang he had tamed. The rumors will grow, but his achievements would become a matter of record: a general at the age of twenty six, scourge of both the Spanish and the Americans, the Republic's single most successful fund raiser.

Yet none of these accomplishments would be as important as the day in June when, with his eyes on the new Philippine flag, General Jose Ignacio Paua cut off his queue. That there were not one, but *two* lengths of black, braided hair that hit the earth on that very first Independence Day, is a fact that is, like the identities of many of the revolution's unsung heroes, lost to history.

FIDELIS TAN *used to be editor of the* Philippine Online Chronicles *(thepoc.net). She has also written stuff for* After the Storm: Stories on Ondoy, *and* Contemporary Art Philippines Magazine.

*Her fiction has appeared in anthologies like* Philippine Speculative Fiction, *vol. 5 and* Spindle *(spindle.ph). She has also collaborated with artists on comics projects such as* Love and Heartbreak, *and the* Quarterly Bathroom Companion Comics Compendium.

*She would now like to direct you to* InTheGrayworld *(inthegrayworld.wordpress.com).*

# The Stranger at my Grandmother's Wake

## Fidelis Tan

ON THE LAST day of my life, I woke up twenty minutes earlier than I usually did—the sky was still dark out the window, although I could hear people moving around outside—the nurses making their rounds, the janitors sweeping the halls. It just came to me that this was the day I would die. There was no fear, or denial. I'd been waiting for years.

At 8:00, the nurse came in with breakfast. She was this tall, pretty girl, who spoke with a bright smile.

She shoveled something warm and mushy into my mouth, and talked about what one of the other caretakers had said. She liked to talk, and I liked her.

In the middle of what she was saying, a small child ran down the corridor, right past my open door.

"Did you see that?" I asked.

She looked up as the child ran back down in the opposite direction, in a flash of orange dress and swinging braids.

"Oh that. Her family's visiting the man next door," she said.

I'd been here over five years, and I had no inkling who my

neighbors were. Something about seeing other old people just reminded me how old I was myself.

"Good for him," I muttered. And although I hadn't planned on telling her, I said, "I'm expecting a visitor today too."

Of course she didn't believe me. "You've never had a visitor before, *Ama*."

"But still," I said. "He told me he'd come early."

"Your husband?"

"I never had a husband," I reminded her. "There was someone a long time ago, but he's probably dead now."

"Finally getting some visitors from the Philippines then?" she asked.

"That's unlikely," I said. "But he should be dropping by to see me. You see, I'm going to die today."

She looked up, surprised.

"I'm sure of it," I said. "I'll pass away, and the man in white will mourn me."

The nurse decided I was joking. "Now, *Ama*," she said. "I know you're not one of the senile ones."

"I'm not. I'm just telling you now so you won't be surprised later," I laid a withered hand on her arm.

The creases between her eyebrows deepened, so I decided I had to explain.

"I first met him a long, long time ago," I said. "This was back in the old country, in Bacolod. That's my grandmother's province. I met him during my grandmother's wake."

It's strenuous, dredging up old memories, and even when you've pulled them out they tend to be murky and brittle. "It was the last time our whole family got together. The whole family."

MY GRANDMOTHER HAD seven children and they all came, with their spouses, and their children. They came from Manila, California, Hong Kong and Vancouver—all the miscellaneous cousins and uncles and aunts, even the ones who had fallen out of touch for one reason or another.

The black sheep came—the family members we all whispered about when their backs were turned. There was my cousin who came out of the closet when he was seventeen, sauntering in with a boyfriend and never once making eye contact with his family. And there was my aunt whose husband had died the year before, and who rumor had it was already several hundred thousand pesos in debt. Even this one cousin who had been at the wrong end of a court case, and had been in hiding over the last few years, managed to show up.

If I had known that I would be a black sheep one day too, I would have been a lot nicer to them. But I was just twenty-two then, arriving with my parents, because I still lived with them at the time. We were fresh off the plane from Manila.

I remember being grumpy because I didn't actually want to attend the funeral—I had never known my grandmother very well. But when you enter a room full of people you resemble to some degree, the same dark hair and dark eyes, all in the white of mourning, you get that sense that it's your duty to be there.

At the wake, I sat with cousin Efren (second son of my father's eldest sister), Joan (my father's fourth brother's daughter) and Michael (the bastard son of my father's youngest brother; we didn't like to talk about his mother, but we liked him well enough).

Efren, Joan, Michael and I were all born on the same year, so it was natural we were always together during these family reunions. We got along well enough, talking about how strict our parents were, and how we'd move out of our houses soon, and live independently and work all day and drink all night. I remember thinking the only good thing about the wake was that I'd get to spend time with them.

We were at the door, accepting donations from the uncles and aunts. They'd sneak wads of thousand-peso bills into our hands, and we'd write their names and the corresponding amount on white ribbons to be put up on the wall. The ribbons were tacked vertically so you could read the Chinese names from top to bottom.

I was writing down a donation for ₱25,000 from an Uncle Hermann—he didn't have a Chinese name so I was just writing his name as is, and thinking how funny it would look with the letters sideways, alongside the columns of Chinese symbols—when Michael spotted the man in white.

It wasn't that he was in white. We were all in white. It wasn't that we couldn't recognize him either. He could have been any of those random people who claimed some connection or the other to our dead grandmother.

But there was something subtly off about him, standing half-hidden behind a large arrangement of wilted orchids from the teacher's organization my grandmother had been part of. He was a bit taller and a bit paler than everyone else, with stringy black hair that fell to his shoulders, and a slight hunch like he had a weight on his back.

He didn't look Filipino or Chinese, but you could easily convince yourself he was either, if you stared at his face long enough.

I caught my mother by the arm as she walked past.

"Who's that?" I asked.

She furrowed her brow. My mother prided herself in knowing every single branch and twig that sprouted from my father's family tree. When I saw her lip twitch, I realized she had absolutely no idea who he was.

"Why don't you ask him?" she asked.

I was about to protest, but she gave me a stern look.

"You only ever talk to these three," she said gesturing towards my cousins. "How do you expect to go through life like that? Go, you have to be more outgoing!"

The words shut in her throat as the man brushed past her shoulder. It didn't look like he heard—he was heading towards the coffin.

I went after him.

Before my grandmother's remains, he stopped and wept. I'd been seeing people do this all day, but always with a hint of prudence—hiding behind a handkerchief, keeping their faces to the ground. But the man was making all these slow, choking noises, the glare of the candelabras beside the coffin casting a yellow sheen on his face, and on the lines the tears made across his cheeks. People were turning to stare.

"You must have known my grandmother well," I said.

He was wiping tears from his eyes. "I met her once," he said.

"Ahh… Friend of hers?"

I glanced over his shoulder, at my mother and cousins. They were all watching intently too.

"Long ago," he said. And then he started crying even harder, inconsolable. I figured I wouldn't get another word in so I slowly edged away.

"So who was he?" My mother asked.

I shrugged. "Friend of *Ama*'s. From long ago."

We passed the word around that he was indeed some friend of our grandmother's, but as the night wore on, all sorts of theories began cropping up.

Maybe he was a student at the school where my grandmother taught in, said my father, as mourners inched around the weeping man, trying to catch a glimpse of my grandmother's stony face in the coffin.

Maybe he was the son of one of my long-dead grandfather's friends, from Canton, whispered an aunt, as monks from the local Chinese temple came to perform the wake rites, with incense and sonorous chanting.

Or maybe he's just an imposter, here for the food, said another uncle, as a priest from the parish celebrated Catholic mass.

But the same thought seemed to pass through me and my three cousins when we exchanged glances—he was none of those.

Dinner time came. He had brought a stir to the wake, but the man in white didn't seem to know anyone else around, so I was obliged to invite him to sit at our table, even if Efren eyed him suspiciously and Michael grew quiet.

The man was polite enough though. He had a plate of *pancit*, fish fillet, barbeque and a little saucer of coffee jelly. He gave us a name when we asked for one—I can't remember it now—but the feeling remained that there was something strange about him.

After food came the beer. The moment the alcohol went down, Joan started cracking stupid jokes and then we were all laughing, even the man in white.

We talked about many things, because it's a wake and no one likes a quiet wake. We did ask the man about himself: his family, what he did for a living, where he came from. I think he mentioned something about having a brother, but I could just be making that up.

Truth is there wasn't much we learned about him, except that he had gone to Bacolod specifically to see my grandmother off, just because they had been friends.

"Friends are important, you see." He said. "They come and go, but the moments you spend together remain."

"That's not true," I said, speaking openly now, like this man was just another one of my cousins. I'd had three, maybe four bottles.

"You keep memories of your friends, but even the memory changes. You forget what they actually said, so you just fill in the gaps. Sometimes you just completely make up what they said, so you say 'weren't we talking about this,' and your friend will say 'no, we never talked about that.'"

"That's true," he said, with a tiny smile that remained on his face as the night wore on.

We didn't realize that most of the family had drifted away, back to the funeral parlor, or off home. I just looked up from behind our growing collection of beer bottles and realized we were the only ones left in the little patio outside the funeral parlor, only the candle on our table left burning against the night. It gave me a chill.

But then Joan cracked another joke—something that made even Michael guffaw into his drink— and I dived right back into the conversation.

Midnight passed us by. Joan and Michael had to go back home with the rest of her family. For a couple more hours it was me, Efren, and the stranger, with Efren regaling us with stories of how he had three different girlfriends, none of whom knew about the others. But right as the moon began to disappear into the horizon, Efren just froze in the middle of a story about how he lost his virginity during a school retreat, and keeled over the side of the table fast asleep.

The man and I both laughed over that for a full five minutes.

"Don't you need to go too?" he finally asked. I had decided by then that he had a pleasant face, with little dimples that appeared at the corner of his mouth when he talked.

"It's my and Efren's families' turn to stay with *Ama* overnight," I said. "There's a little room at the back of the parlor where people can sleep and take a shower and things."

The moon had disappeared behind the trees, and I realized I was alone with the stranger.

"How did you say you met my grandmother again?" I asked in a small voice.

"It was around five, six decades ago," he said.

"But how can that be?" I was slurring all over my words, but the man didn't even seem tipsy. "You don't look much older than me."

"I'm older than I look," he said pleasantly. "I'm old and I've been everywhere, but I never forget the people I meet."

"Like your grandmother," he said. "It was in a little town, not too far from here."

I rested my head down on the table, but still with my eyes on him. His eyes had lit up, talking about my grandmother. It sent a peculiar flush creeping up my face, which had nothing to do with the beer.

"IT WAS DURING a different wake," he told me. "But not like this. It was a lonely one. Imagine a tiny church, and inside, the coffin, and before it, a single figure on his knees, wailing like there'd be no tomorrow. That was me."

"Your grandmother came in with two of her friends. They had heard me crying and came to see what was happening. When they saw that a wake was in order, they decided it would be rude not to inquire who the dead was."

"'A dear friend,' I said. 'Whom I haven't seen in many years.'"

"Your grandmother took a look around the church and asked, where's the family? Dead, during the war. Where are the neighbors? The neighbors informed the undertaker of her passing and took that to be the end of their obligation."

"Now, this seemed to ruffle your grandmother a great deal. So who'll say the prayers, and eat and drink at the wake, and drop flowers into the grave? I told her I suppose I would. I could tell from the way she looked right then, that she had made up her mind about something."

"'We'll help you,' she said. One of her friends began to raise an argument—something along the line of them not knowing me, or the deceased, but your grandmother was a strong-willed woman."

"She told her friends they could leave if they wanted to, but in the end they decided to stick around, if just to make sure she wasn't alone with me."

"So then there were four of us, reciting the prayers, and then passing around a bottle of watered-down gin, and telling stories. Your grandmother began to weep for the dead as well. She told me that it was a Chinese custom to get people to cry at wakes, even if the criers themselves didn't know the dead. She told me that her fiancée, a Chinese man, had told her this."

"It was a bit funny, seeing her cry for someone she didn't know, and her friends, who had nothing better to do, decided to cry along. My tears were sincere, but I couldn't hide how happy I was to have them with me there."

"We were at it a while until the priest came to say the final rites, and the body was put in the ground, under a grave that bore no name."

"When it was all over I told them that they had all done me a great, personal kindness—and that in return I would visit each of them, on the day of their funerals."

"AND I KEPT my promise," he said, downing his beer.

"The first died in the sixties, in an unfortunate accident. The second grew sick and died in a hospital. And then there's your grandmother," he said. "Who married her Chinese man and had many children and grandchildren."

The man in white gave me a sad smile then. "I'm happy to be here too. To give her honor, and to have met all of you."

"You must've met a lot of people," I said softly.

"I have," he agreed. "It's very rare that I meet the same person more than once, but it shames me to think of all the time we may have spent together. So I make up for it by mourning them when they pass away."

He was looking right at me. "First comes death, and then me."

I laughed, mostly to break his gaze. "But that's just stupid," I said. "Why leave? Why don't you just stay, make some real friends?"

"It would be complicated," he said. "I can't stay in one place too long."

"So you don't even keep in touch? How will you even know when I die?"

"I'll know," he said.

"Well, you better come early, at least," I said. "So we can talk before I die. Promise me that."

"I can make that promise, but I don't know if I can keep it," he looked up thoughtfully. "But I'll try."

At that moment, Efren murmured in his sleep, so we figured it was best to get him indoors. The stranger and I hoisted him up, one arm each over our shoulders, and half-walked, half-dragged him back into the funeral parlor.

After that I might have just passed out as well. When morning came the stranger was gone, and I had the most spectacular headache I had ever experienced.

THE NURSE LAUGHED at that.

"What?" I asked. "You don't think I couldn't drink my weight in beer?"

"I don't doubt you could, *Ama*," she said, clearing away the dishes and preparing my daily medicine.

"Did you ever see him again?" she asked.

"No. But If I had stayed at home, I may have caught him again."

Before me she set a line of pills, all of which I had to take. There was a big white pill, a small rounded blue pill, and a powdery green one, which I always had trouble swallowing. Sitting in a row like that, they reminded me of my three cousins.

"A few years after my *Ama* was put into the earth, my cousin Michael killed himself," I told the nurse, as I popped the white pill into my mouth. "They found him strung up from a pipe in the bathroom. He had always been a sad boy, I guess no one knew just how sad. I was on vacation with my parents when I heard he was dead. We would have gone to his funeral, but his parents didn't even give him a proper wake. Just held a brief service and had him cremated. Efren was in Hong Kong at the time."

"Joan got to see him though, before they burned the remains. 'Guess who was there,' she told me over the phone. 'The man from Ama's wake. He looks exactly like he did before,' she said. I asked her where he'd gone, but she had no idea, and somehow I wasn't surprised."

Next went the blue pill, downed with a swish of water from a plastic cup.

"A few years later Efren died in a plane crash. The XF-740 tragedy. Ever heard of that? No, it was before your time. His body was never recovered, so we just held a mass for him."

"I waited for the man in white to show up but he never did—but just as I figured he wasn't so big on keeping his promises after all, it occurred to me that maybe it was because Efren—his body anyway, wasn't really there. I had this distinct vision of the man in white kneeling over Efren's corpse, wherever it might have washed up. Maybe some lonely island, or some rock out in the sea. I imagined the man in white on his knees over whatever remained of Efren's face, crying like he did for my grandmother."

I took a good long look at the green pill. I think it was to regulate my heart, or my circulation. Either way, this was the last time I'd ever have to take it.

"Joan died in the Philippines," I said, playing with the pill between my fingers. "I like to think she had it best, out of all of us. She died of sickness, but she was with her husband and kids. At least that's what I heard."

I took the green pill with a wince. It always left a bitter taste in my mouth.

"I loved Joan like a sister, but there was no way I was going back to the Philippines, even to see her off," I said.

I left it at that, but the memories had come rising up to greet me. At the time Joan died, I was already living in Canada, with the man I generally passed off as my husband.

I found out over the Internet that Joan had passed away. It was the only time I considered calling anyone from my family. I wanted to ask if the man in white had visited—if he still looked exactly the same as before. In the end, I didn't.

"I am looking forward to seeing my friend," I said to the nurse. "If he gets here before I die."

The nurse smiled in an indulgent way. "You shouldn't be talking about that, *Ama*," the nurse said. "Talking about death's bad luck."

"I'm all out of use for luck. I'm old."

"You've got plenty to live for." She gestured out the window. "You see the sky today? All blue with puffy white clouds? That's a day worth living for."

Maybe for you, I wanted to say. My eyes were still good, but I'd seen enough pretty skies.

"What do you people do here, when someone dies?" I asked.

"We inform your family—"

"Assume I have no family," I said. "Or that they're too far away to care, which is pretty much the same thing."

"Well," she shrugged. "What we used to do was we'd bury the body—we have this plot out back. But the plot's full so now we just cremate the remains and give the ashes to the wind."

"Will there be a funeral?" I asked. "A wake?"

She hesitated. "We can hold a service, if you want," she drew back the curtains as far as they went, to make sure I didn't miss out on the nice blue sky.

"If I wanted to have a wake, would you attend?" I asked.

She didn't answer. I could tell she was just pretending she couldn't hear me, but I let it go.

I hadn't always known I'd be dying on my own, but when it occurred to me that I would, I accepted it. There'd never be a great big funeral feast for me, no prayers, no mourners—just the man in white to shed a few tears on my behalf.

I WAS IN my thirties when it first dawned upon me that I could very well die alone. That's when I finally left home. My mother had called me every single foul name she could think of—and I had called her a few in return. My father wasn't speaking to me at all, which was worse.

It wouldn't have been so bad if it was just a matter of falling in love. True, he was Filipino, and my family had never been comfortable admitting full-blooded Filipinos into the fold. But that could have been worked on. My grandmother was Filipino after all. The real trouble was that he was twenty-five years my senior, and at the time, married with children.

Of course I didn't see that. I only saw that he was my way out of the family at long last. He even looked like the man in white, a little bit, although I never told him that.

He ended up leaving his family for me, so I did too. It made sense to me—we were two broken pieces making a whole.

I may have been crying when I climbed into the taxi that would take me away, but as we began rolling down the curb, and I got that distinct feeling I was leaving everything behind, I grew resolute. I told myself that I would never turn back.

Even then, I kept looking out the window, wishing I'd see the man in white. I wasn't dead, but I had something to mourn, and I needed someone to mourn with me.

The further I got from home, the lighter it felt, at least at the time. My lover and I would eventually run away to Canada, so I would never get further away from my family than that.

BUT THEN HE asked me to marry him.

We had gone to Whistler, where the snow had turned the mountains into postcards and younger people were dragging their skis through knee-deep sludge. We had dinner on a breezy veranda overlooking the yard, the light from a standing brazier making the shadows around his eyes and mouth deeper. Right in the middle of dessert he dropped down on a knee and proposed—ring and all.

The other vacationers stopped and stared, some cheering, some actually clapping their hands. I was rigid in my seat, looking down at him, at his sureness. It made my blood boil.

I said no. As his face fell, I made a realization—all this time I had mistaken the feeling of lightness for emptiness; and out here, a cold wind was screaming through my bones.

After that it was just a matter of when he would leave, and I could ease myself into the cycle of living alone, working all day, drinking all night. It wasn't a bad way to spend thirty-seven years.

But the grayer my hair got, and the creakier my joints, the longer I'd spend looking out of windows, of buses and buildings and hospitals, watching the people who passed by, who disappeared out the corner of my vision, hoping one of them was the man in white. I never saw him.

One day life was waking up at 8:00 in the morning with a sweet lady nurse bringing me breakfast, and taking my pills, and then just sitting, and remembering—and there was already too much I couldn't remember.

THE SUN WAS beginning to set. The shadows of the window grills grew long across the covers of my bed, over the little hills my legs made under the blanket.

Soon, I thought. The man in white would visit, and then I would die, or vice-versa. It didn't matter, I thought, what happened after.

Maybe I'd see my cousins again, I thought. Poor, sad Michael. Loud, laughing Efren. Joan and all her funny stories.

Or maybe I'd just drift into a long, dreamless sleep. That was what I was hoping for the most, actually.

I chanced to look outside—the sun had dipped behind the big elm they had in the hospital yard, the glare peeking through, so the leaves were on fire.

And then I saw the little girl in the orange dress had somehow ended up in the yard, her braids twitching when she moved her head. She was looking up, talking to a stranger dressed all in white.

My heart leapt. Could it be him?

I couldn't see his face. He had gotten on one knee so he could talk to the little girl face to face. What was he telling her, I wondered. Was he telling her how good it was to talk to someone like her? That one day, far into the future, he'd mourn her brief, fragile life?

I watched them until my neck began to ache trying to see them through the glare. I leaned back against the pillows. He'd come up eventually, to see me. How wonderful it would be to open my arms in greeting when he came through the door. Old friend, I'd say. My only friend left.

I closed my eyes for a moment, and in that darkness I knew that what he said before was true. He only really got to meet people once , and next he'd be mourning them. Except for Joan, I thought. He got to talk to her at Michael's service right? But suddenly I wasn't sure. The past had grown dim, the people in them were all silhouettes on a dark screen, and I was so very tired.

I'll take a nap, I decided, burrowing my hands up to the elbows under the blankets. I turned away from the light, the pillow's fabric rough on the side of my face. I imagined I was hearing footsteps in the hall.

MARC GREGORY Y. YU *graduated from the University of the Philippines and is currently enjoying the thrill of being a newly-licensed doctor. Once in a while, he leaves the portals of science to traverse the very fine line between the real and the unreal. His works have appeared in the* Philippines Graphic, *the* Philippine Daily Inquirer, *and* Tulay Fortnightly Magazine. *He received a Palanca award in 2004 and a Philippines Graphic-Nick Joaquin Literary Award in 2010.*

# Chopsticks

## Marc Gregory Yu

*The honorable and upright man keeps well away from both the slaughterhouse and the kitchen. And he allows no knives on his table.*

-CONFUCIUS-

THE PAIR OF green porcelain chopsticks neatly sliced through the air in a perfect arc, momentarily stopping midway before giving off one pliant sweeping motion to land straight on Mother's enormous, half-eaten plate.

"Genuine porcelain. Fifty bucks," Mother bragged in a singsong voice, her gleaming, slit-like eyes peering out from behind thick spectacles as she held out the two slender objects for everyone else to get a better look. Like all typical Chinese chopsticks, they are blunted at both ends—square in cross section at one end (where they are held by the fingers) and round at the other. The color is a deep, celadon green, with varying shades of bamboo shoots sprouting out across the lacquered surface. With each closer look, the shoots seemed to come alive in the lamplight, glistening with the quality of burnished wood.

Truth be told, however, Mother's statement could not come across as more unbelievable. Wooden chopsticks are a dime a dozen and can be had for only a few pennies each, but not porcelain chopsticks. Not a pair as magnificent, polished, and exquisite as these, or at least that's what Mother claimed them to be.

I watched her twirl the chopsticks with remarkable dexterity, caressing one end with her delicate fingers and smoothing the other with a piece of cloth. Earlier that day, she had gone down the street to buy *ganmaopian* for my grandmother's ailing cough. The old woman was awake coughing her lungs out all night, and from my room I could hear our spinster neighbor groaning from all the noise. Grandma had refused antibiotics, saying her zodiac sign forbade her to drink that "funny-smelling orange liquid" if she wanted her luck element intact. Father feared it might be tuberculosis, but Mother simply called it the result of playing too much mahjong. All the same, our neighbor's early morning complaint sent her trudging along to the huge herbal store on the other side of the street, and was about to turn around the corner when the sight of something stopped her short.

"From the looks of it, she was new here. Unlike those pretty ladies in 168 who will pester you endlessly with their ridiculous offers, this one was a rather modest-looking woman. She was huddled along the sidewalk, wearing a coat twice her size, though the weather's not exactly freezing if you'd ask me. Her goods were laid out on a shiny crimson rug, and she was sort of staring into space. Was she lonely? Homesick? Thinking of her husband? For heaven's sake, I do not know. All the same, she didn't notice me approaching until I inquired about this…this piece of treasure."

She put the chopsticks to her thin lips and kissed them gently.

When I was five, I thought chopsticks were an absolute pain in the neck. The first time I held them, they kept slipping from my fingers, and I fumbled about gripping them awkwardly, each stick bumping into the other every time I twisted them in the wrong direction. Mother always made it look so easy. The chopsticks would lithely rise in her hands as she directed them into a plate of steaming noodles, securely clipping a reasonable amount and bringing them to her plate—or straight to her mouth.

"You have to hold them like tongs," she demonstrated. "And by all means, grasp them firmly. You don't want to end up with nothing." It was understandably a test of control and coordination, and somewhere at the back of my head I recalled her narrating that five thousand years of practice that made China home of the world's best surgeons, her voice swelling with pride.

This time, however, her voice was one of pure delight, like a child who had just unearthed the discovery of a lifetime.

"Of course she wouldn't let me have it for a mere fifty! Genuine porcelain, see. And you have to admit, times are hard these days. But my haggling skills finally went right through her in the end. Turned out she was new here, after all. And from *Jinjiang*—would you believe it? When I excitedly told her we might even be distant cousins, you should have seen how her eyes lit up—"

"—and you didn't even realize she's probably a phony."

We were too eagerly awaiting the next part of the story to notice that Grandma was the only one who remained silent all this time. She had one eyebrow raised, arms folded across her chest, and lips pouted in the direction of the purring ceiling fan.

"And I'll tell you why."

She leaned forward, scooped the chopsticks from Mother (who suddenly looked bewildered) and scrutinized them up close, so close they almost hit the bridge of her nose.

"They feel coarse," she frowned, kneading them between her wrinkled fingers. "Real, genuine porcelain is flawlessly smooth, the texture of flowing water. And pardon me, but these sticks don't seem to contain any measure of *chi* at all. Nothing! What makes you so sure about that woman? From what I see here, I bet you she's another one of those crooked impostors who feast themselves on monkey business. Know what happens to them? They get shipped back to where they rightfully belong. Any feng shui master will prove to you your chopsticks are fake."

The last sentence made Mother's expression turn awry, as if in painful reminiscence of a tragic past. Three years ago, a geomancer visited our home and saw Mother's elegant wooden Shanghainese chopsticks (which she had purchased on a trip the year before) displayed atop the grand piano. They were artistic masterpieces in their own right, sporting glossy miniature paintings of Peking opera masks amid a background of cerulean blue. Mother was thoroughly fascinated the moment she spied them peeking out of some little antique shop along a busy stretch of Nanking Road. She had to pay an arm and a leg, but no matter. The thought of her leaving Shanghai without them was simply unthinkable.

The geomancer surveyed the entire living room from every angle, occasionally making measurements, his lips muttering a series of strange incantations as he paced to and fro. After several minutes, he finally clapped his hands and politely concluded that the arrangement simply wouldn't do. The piano and chopsticks was interpreted as a gigantic overturned rice bowl with the chopsticks poking straight up—definitely a magnet for misfortune to befall the house and its constituents. It was thus proposed that Mother place the chopsticks atop the oven instead, to bring positive energy to the kitchen.

At around four in the afternoon the next day, a deafening noise broke out in the kitchen. A slight electrical disturbance had caused the oven to explode. Someone dialed the fire department at once, but when the first fire truck arrived, it was too late. Mother came rushing home from work to find the whole kitchen black with soot and smoke. Her precious chopsticks were nowhere to be found.

That night, Father was surprised to see *Lillian Too's 168 Ways to a Calm and Happy Life* missing from its usual location on the top shelf. *Practical Feng Shui for Daily Living* had disappeared, too, and so with the rest of the other feng shui books in the house. An hour later, we were startled by an unusual crackling noise coming from the backyard. A huge bonfire roared merrily, Mother smugly humming on a chair nearby.

The following day, we were invited over to Mrs. Chan's house where she avidly showed everyone the brand new peach-and-yellow porcelain chopsticks she had acquired in an auction at Sotheby's in Hong Kong. They featured golden prancing peacocks on the surface, and Mrs. Chan boasted of how she successfully defended her bid from her last ardent challenger—a balding Cantonese curator who wanted the chopsticks as the latest addition to his growing museum of peacock collectibles.

The chopsticks were admiringly passed around to the guests, who incessantly heaped tons of praises on the owner for having secured such a rare treasure. When it was finally Mother's turn, however, no words emerged from her dry lips. Her face was twisted into an excruciating grimace camouflaged by a weak smile that presumably took a lot of effort to produce. Before I knew it, she had feigned a bout of stomach pain, apologized to everyone for the momentary distraction, thanked Mrs. Chan for her generosity, grabbed me by the cuff of my shirt, and marched off to the car without another word.

Mother was wearing the same agonizing expression when Grandma's unforeseen statement struck her like a spear. Her eyes had a cloudy look about them, and for a few minutes she was deep in her thoughts, as if searching for a possible gap in the old woman's words.

"I don't believe it, "she began slowly, shaking her head. "Not any of this rubbish. I remember you telling me about how Mrs. Chan supposedly got herself a bogus pair. The type of material, no *chi* at all—you expect me to believe any of these things? For goodness' sake, she legally purchased them from a reputable institution! And lest you forget, her daughter who manages a curio shop has quite confirmed that the chopsticks were indeed genuine. You speak of *chi*? That is all a piece of nonsense." Mother haughtily twitched her nose after finishing the last sentence.

"Which only means," she placed the chopsticks in the middle of the table. "That there is no need to contradict. I am most certainly sure they are genuine."

"*Aya*, but just so you know, you do not get hold of genuine porcelain chopsticks for fifty bucks!" Grandma cried out, largely unconvinced. "Think about it! And with that daughter of hers!"

Grandma was referring to no other than the fateful incident that took place forty days after Grandpa's demise. Being close family friends, the Chans came over for dinner in commemoration of the occasion. All was going well. Father and Mr. Chan were in high spirits, exchanging views on the revised government bill mandating the new registration process for Chinese aliens. Mrs. Chan was graciously complimenting Mother's hot-and-sour soup, begging for a copy of the recipe (*"I can never make it quite as well as you do!"*). Grandma, on the other hand, remained oblivious to all these, contentedly groping about with a toothpick.

Then all of a sudden the daughter absentmindedly stuck her chopsticks straight up in her bowl of rice, similar to what was earlier offered before Grandpa's enormous toothless picture in the hall. Obviously, she had no idea of the terrible faux pas committed, or she would have corrected herself punctiliously. The whole table was instantly thrown into chaos. Father almost choked on a walnut; Mother cupped her hands to her mouth; and the Chans glared at their daughter with mouths agape, as if having witnessed her carry out a grisly murder right before their very eyes. As for Grandma—well, we were horrified to see her go ghastly white, and feared she might topple over her chair anytime.

But Grandma didn't seem intent on reliving any more horror stories, for the meantime. She stood up from the table and proceeded to the huge mahogany cabinet where she kept all her memorabilia. She fumbled in one of the drawers that had a rusty keyhole and drew out a pair of dirty, ungainly chopsticks wrapped in a piece of yellowing paper. A thick coat of dust had settled on the surface, and she blew on them lightly.

I had seen those chopsticks before. Grandma kept clutching them tightly the night we ran out of chopsticks for Grandpa's guests, and she had indignantly refused Mother's request to let good old Mr. Chao use them.

"Things like these have no place on the dining table!" she furiously snapped.

Mother could only scratch her head, apparently confused. But she had no time to argue or even discuss the logic of Grandma's words. Left with no other choice, she had to hurry out into the street and scour for any stores that might still be open, and that sold chopsticks. Fortunately, the crisis was resolved in the nick of time. By the time dinner was over Grandma had considerably cooled down and even insisted Mr. Chao play a round of mahjong with her instead.

Grandma was now carefully unwrapping the paper, spreading it out on the table for everyone to see. Though at first the outlines were blurred, I was gradually able to make out the contents of a short message written with *mao bi*, the ink somewhat smudged but the words otherwise clear:

*To Xiaoping and Meilin,*
> *Happiness and joy on your life as one,*
> *And the gods bless you with a healthy son.*
> > *Chen Xiaoling*
> > *08 / 1950*

Everyone intently read the letter, but from the corner of my eye I could see that Grandma was teary-eyed with emotion. She was looking past the neatly unfolded piece of paper laid before us, as if it contained something else other than the mere words etched on its surface.

"Your Grandpa and I were married at the height of the Communist Revolution. He was a brilliant scholar, and both the Communists and the Kuomintang wanted him on their side and sought ways to recruit him. But he was a peaceful man; didn't want to have anything to do with the war even though I am sure he had read Sun Tzu's *The Art of War* at least a hundred times. So he decided that the best way for us was to flee the country."

She pointed to her wobbly feet.

"You might wonder why I never had bound feet. Can you imagine? For as long as I am not in my grave, I shall hear nothing of it. I locked myself in the attic when I knew my father was planning to let the town matchmaker bind my feet and have them curl up like a lotus blooming in the pond. Everyone believes that is the measure of beauty; I believe it's to keep us imprisoned in the house, to be reduced to second-rate creatures who could only limp along when all the others could run like the wind. Fearing humiliation, my parents initially tried to keep it a secret, to no avail. The villagers eventually discovered what happened, and my family was forever disgraced. My mother threw me out in a fit of anger. Whenever I passed any of the townsfolk, they jeered at me and branded me *xiao xiong guei*, the little witch-demon. Naturally, no one wanted me for a wife. I was lucky to have found shelter in the home of my friend Xiaoling."

She breathed deeply, trying to regain composure.

"Luckier still, to have met someone who truly loved me for who I was—her brother, your grandfather."

So now it all made sense. Many times in the middle of the night, I would sneak downstairs to find Grandma fully awake, writing letters and wrapping packages. Certainly, they weren't for any of her family members back in China; she had informed us they were long dead, poisoned by tradition. Instead, the fruits of her labor were for a dear "friend," without whom, she explained, none of us would be alive today. Back then I thought she was only being too metaphoric.

"I will never forget that day. It was the Mid-Autumn Festival and the moon was full. An auspicious sign, I tell you. Everything was ready. We had it all planned out. A boat loaded with cargo was set to sail for the Philippines, and the owner was Xiaoling's good friend who agreed to let us in on one condition: We must leave without a trace. Xiaoling was there up to the very moment our boat sailed out to sea. Before I embarked, she ran up to me and hugged me tightly. Then she reached into her pocket and pulled out a pair of chopsticks wrapped in paper. She told me to take them."

Slowly, Grandma raised one bony finger to the words written on the paper. They seemed to burn with memory.

"In those days, chopsticks symbolize a lot of things. For a newly married couple, in particular, the gift of chopsticks is an earnest appeal to heaven, a humble prayer to the gods for a firstborn son. But that is only looking at it from the shallowest perspective. For someone who has journeyed a thousand miles just to reach a new lease on life, they represent many other, more important things. Friendship. Courage. Trust. Freedom. Hope. And...undying love."

The silence at the table was unnerving. Father was evidently uneasy at this sudden, unexpected revelation of a juicy chunk of family history, especially since my grandparents had fittingly named him *"kuai zi"* (chopsticks) in honor of the objects that allegedly brought him to existence. Just as Grandma reached the part of the firstborn son, "Chopsticks" uncomfortably gave a little squirm, and now his gaze intermittently shifted from a narrow crack on the floor to a speckled house gecko now pursuing a bug on the wall. I chuckled silently in my seat, greatly amused to see Father regressing back to being a child.

Mother, for her part, had stopped fiddling her chopsticks and her eyes lolled; she appeared to be deep in some sort of trance. We siblings were a confluence of puzzled looks composed of the same helpless, speechless faces—my sister greatly taken aback, my brother looking somewhat at a loss. And then it suddenly hit me: All her life, Grandma never bothered to learn using a spoon and fork.

It seemed her staunch belief in the superiority of chopsticks only intensified every time someone courteously suggested it's about time she learned the stuff of modern times. Father was exceptionally persistent. Over breakfast, lunch, and dinner, and always with a mischievous twinkle in his eye, he would instinctively let out charming little snippets like "Come on, Ma, don't you think it's a bit unsanitary?" whenever Grandma tried poking at meat morsels with her chopsticks, or if she found it difficult to pick up the last grains of rice on her plate, "Using a spoon and fork would make things easier, really now..."

Unfortunately, in the end, even Father was forced to desist. The old woman proved too strong-willed. Grandma was born under the Year of the Dragon, and she was notorious as a living, breathing ball of fire. Back in her younger years, Grandpa once recounted of the night she subdued a burglar with her bare hands after making out his silhouette stealthily moving in the shadows. Reeling from her blows, the reluctant burglar fell unconscious, sustaining major injuries, and had to be lifted by an ambulance to the nearest hospital. My aunts and uncles deemed it a foolish mistake to mess with her, and so I thought Father should know better whenever he attempted to cajole her with one or another of his fancy remarks.

"Shut up if you don't know what's good for you!"

"You are going to speak no more of such things, do you understand?"

"*Utensils*? You say they are utensils? That is downright denigration of a piece of art, of a way of life!"

It never mattered whether Grandma had finished eating or not. Furious, her healthy appetite would completely vanish into thin air, and she would promptly stand up, stomp to her room and slam the door behind her. That would be the last we heard of her.

Father was in no state to disturb the old woman's pensive mood today, not after he was unwillingly given a piece of the puzzle to his own personal beginnings. After an unbearably long minute, seeing no one bothered to make a sound, he offered to break the monotony by suggesting we invite Mrs. Chan's daughter for dinner, just to let her have a look at Mother's chopsticks, but Grandma was the first to object—vehemently at that. She wanted no more sacrilege.

"What I am trying to tell you is that these chopsticks mean absolutely nothing to me. If you insist that they are genuine, so be it. They are worthless anyway. "

And she stifled a yawn, hastily stowed back the message and her dirty chopsticks and strode straight to her room without a murmur. She never emerged again for the rest of the evening.

"The cough is getting to her head," Mother quietly explained, taking away her new chopsticks and shaking her head each time a guttural noise issued from within Grandma's room, accompanied by the grouchy mumble of someone wont to toss and turn in bed. But from the look on her face, I could tell that Mother was visibly bothered. She immediately took to the dishes and reminded us of schoolwork, pretending not to hear our next-door neighbor who had also begun her own cycle of tossing and turning, hurling crass expletives at an unspecified target for her wretched sleeplessness.

That night, Mother surprised us all with a change of heart. She planned to sell the chopsticks the very next day. "I couldn't bear to see them break," she reasoned, saying they were "too fragile" for her taste.

When our store opened the following morning, I found that the chopsticks had been placed on a most strategic location. They stood out eminently at the center of the front row, the distinctive celadon green with bamboo shoots glinting in the sunlight, a striking contrast from the rest of the merchandise on sale. A price tag had been conspicuously attached. The cost: forty bucks. Mother herself will see to it that she personally makes the sale. Absolutely no haggling; the price is cheap enough. As potential customers passed by, she began to woo them with the zeal and alacrity of someone twenty years younger.

"Genuine porcelain, forty bucks!"

Her singsong voice caught the attention of several amused passersby, but at the very most they only took a second look at the chopsticks before reciprocating Mother's wide-cheeked, gracious smile. An hour after, however, I discovered that she was staring blankly into space. She didn't even notice a modest-looking woman come up and inquire about the chopsticks, wearing a coat twice her size, the swirling green of the chopsticks now looking chipped off in the light.

YVETTE TAN *is an award-winning horror author whose lifestyle writing includes food, travel, fashion, beauty and personalities—nothing like her stories at all. She is currently working on her novel while continuing to freelance for various publications, as well as being writer-at-large for* Esquire Philippines.

# Fold Up Boy

## Yvette Tan

KAT LIM SAW him again. He had been flitting in and out of her vision, an apparition, a boy about her age who dressed as if he had come out of a Chinese period movie.

He started following her around after she opened her locker and he tumbled out, unfolding like badly-made *zhezhi*, the ancient Chinese paper art that her grandmother liked to construct. He was a ragged mess, clothes dirtied with mud and blood, smelling of soil and gore, hair matted and falling out of his braid, the exposed parts of his arms and legs covered with wounds and gashes, some scabbed, some still bleeding.

Kat stepped back and screamed. She ran off, leaving her bag and locker open, books strewn on the floor. Teachers were called. Kat was found, calmed, and sent home. Her mother had picked her up, tears in her eyes, all apologies. "This is our fault," she said. "You shouldn't have to go through this."

Kat was silent the whole time, even when they got home and her parents pretended to be on good terms for her benefit. She wouldn't tell anyone why she freaked out, and refused to talk or eat until the day after, when she had convinced herself that whatever it was she saw was brought on by stress. By then, her parents' charade was already beginning to wear thin, her mother snapping at her father before remembering their daughter; her father walking past her mother before seeing Kat, then making an effort to say hello to his wife at the dinner table. Their strange dance only served to tire Kat more, so that when the next day came, she was glad to be away from the house.

But he was there when she returned to school—and this time, he was out to find her.

As soon as she stepped on school grounds, she spotted him: a walking wound. His head was bashed in, some of the wet, pulpy mass falling onto his face. His shirt was ragged, dirt rubbed in so much that she didn't know what color it had originally been. He walked around searching for something, going around the pretty girls, ignoring the brains, stepping around the freshmen. Kat mentally thanked her parents for sending her to a Catholic all-girls school that had a uniform that made everyone look like the nuns that ran the institution. *It should take him a while to find me*, she thought, even as she questioned how certain she was that it was her he was after, and why only she could see him. She waited until he passed her friends before heading towards them, brushing away their questions about what happened to her two days before with, "I'm okay now."

Later, she saw him stalking the hallway during class hours, peeking into the rooms. When he poked his head into her classroom she looked away, hoping that he would not recognize the back of her head.

When he didn't show up during recess, she figured that he had gone back to whatever dimension spewed him.

But he popped up in the library, where she liked to go during lunch break when she had to study (read: cram) for a test. She had forgotten about him by then, her fear of the bizarre replaced with a more immediate worry. They had an exam in Chinese language class later that day, and she knew that *lao shi*, their oftentimes ornery teacher, wasn't going to let her off, even though she had just broken down in front of the whole school two days before. Good thing they only had one Chinese class—Kat sucked at the language. What use was studying Mandarin when they were taught to memorize words and stories that had no bearing in the real world? After twelve years in what was loosely termed a "Chinese school," most students, Kat included, hadn't learned much beyond, "Can I go to the bathroom?"

This was why most students took to memorizing their lessons. The ones with better memories generally got better grades. Unfortunately, Kat was not one of them. Even worse, her membership in the school volleyball team depended on her passing all her subjects, Chinese class included.

"It's not like we use it in real life anyway," Kat muttered for the hundredth time while trying to memorize the answer to, "What did the venerable teacher Confucius eat for breakfast?"

It wasn't that she couldn't speak Chinese. She spoke Fookien—the dialect from the Fujian province where most Filipino-Chinese came from—just fine, since that was what her parents used at home, aside from English and Tagalog, which she spoke with her friends. It was the Mandarin she couldn't understand. "Not like I'm going to strike a conversation about Confucius anyway," she grumbled.

A male voice made her jump. She looked up to find the boy staring at her. His clothes were still bloody, but his wounds seemed to have healed, the blood wiped away from his exposed skin. He smelled like a grave, like a boy who refused to die. Kat opened her mouth to scream, but the boy pointed a finger in her direction and the scream caught in her throat.

"Don't be afraid," he said in Fookien, though she could barely make out the words through his thick accent.

He was almost transparent. Behind him, the room was almost empty, with only one or two students milling about. For some reason, this gave her comfort. She relaxed, and was glad that he seemed to sense it too.

"I won't hurt you."

He was dressed in a dirty tunic and pants so old-fashioned even her grandfather refused to wear them. His long hair was kept in a braid that hung low on his back. He looked like an extra in a Jet Li period film, one of those who got beat up, or killed. He dropped his hand. She found her voice.

"What are you?" she asked, also in Fookien, keeping her voice to a whisper.

"My name is Sui Duan," he said.

"Why do you keep following me?" Kat asked.

"I've been looking for my family for so long." He seemed lost then, as if he suddenly realized the absurdity of his situation.

"You know you're dead, right?"

He looked away. "You have to help me find my family."

Kat sighed. "Look," she said. "I don't know why I can see you. And you can't just show up and demand that I help you find your family. If you'll excuse me, I have a test to study for."

Sui Duan glanced at the notes in front of Kat.

"I can help you," he said.

"What?"

"I can help you." He waved at her schoolwork.

The bell rang, signaling the end of lunch hour.

"Forget it," she said in English, gathering her things and getting up.

SHE REGRETTED HER decision later as she stared at the exam in front of her. Their sadistic teacher didn't just give them a quiz. This was a full-fledged exam, thirty questions on three lessons. Sure, she tried to make it "easier" by making it multiple choice, but that didn't help Kat at all, seeing as she hadn't really studied. She cursed Sui Duan for scaring her and making her miss two days of classes, and she cursed *lao shi* for not caring that she had had a breakdown a few days before. She stared at her test paper, watching the characters swim together like broken sticks in water. *Good luck to me.*

She was about to circle a random letter when she smelled what she could only describe as the inside of a slaughterhouse and heard a voice beside her whisper "The third one." She looked up. *Lao shi* was staring at her strangely but did not say anything. Around her, classmates were busy with their own papers. Not that she needed to know who had spoken. There were only two choices. She could flunk this test and fail a subject and not be allowed to play on the team. Or she could accept help from a ghost and be forced to do him a favor.

She circled the C.

"Damn you," she said under her breath.

"Do you want the answer to the next one?"

Kat didn't answer. She needed to pass this exam badly. Failing Chinese meant a summer spent in a stuffy classroom with other students who had failed the subject instead of going to Tokyo Disneyland with her mother. Her parents had been taking her on a lot of trips lately during long weekends and holidays. Sometimes they were all together but more often than not with just one parent. They called it bonding time. Kat knew it was more for their benefit than hers but she enjoyed them anyway.

There was no question about it. She was going to fail this exam without Sui Duan's help. On the other hand, if she let him coach her, that effectively meant acknowledging he was real and helping him in whatever stupid quest he was on. She sighed, nodded her head slightly.

She thought she heard a chuckle. But when he spoke, there was no mistaking the answer to the next question.

SUI DUAN CAME back after volleyball practice, after the other girls went home and it was only Kat who remained. This was normal. Kat would text her mother when it was time to fetch her, and since her mother was coming from the office—and Manila was always jammed with traffic—it usually meant a long wait. Kat didn't mind most of the time. She liked to revel in the serenity, to watch darkness settle over the school.

"So you'll help me."

Kat sighed. "Guess I have no choice."

She stared at him, something that she realized she was afraid to do, limiting her observations to side glances and what she could see from far away.

He was cleaned up now. All the bloodstains were gone, all his wounds healed. Now he really looked like an extra in a kung fu flick. He even had the tiny black shoes. She was surprised to find that he was kind of cute. The words *fold up boy* came to her head, from the first time she saw him tumble out of her locker, like a marionette being unfolded by its master.

"How old are you?" she asked.

Sui Duan gave her a look of surprise. "Sixteen. I was supposed to turn sixteen."

"How?" Kat trailed off, unable to finish the sentence.

Sui Duan looked away, silent.

"If you want me to help you, you have to at least tell me how you got..." she waved her hand "...dead in the first place."

She wondered how many times she was going to have to remind him that he was dead.

"Tell me why a ghost from China is wandering around Manila."

Idly, she thought that she might have to strike up a conversation about the venerable teacher Confucius after all.

Sui Duan seemed to take offense at this. "I didn't. I'm not from China. I was born here."

*You could have fooled me.*

HE SAT BESIDE her on the floor behind the cyclone wire that was supposed to keep the students in and the bad elements out. He looked lost then, more like a little boy who lost his family than someone who was pestering her the whole day. It was hard not to feel sorry for him.

"What happened?"

"They said we were against the government," he whispered. His hands were shaking. She could hear the rage rising in his voice, getting stronger as he spat out each syllable. "We only wanted to live safely, in our own home, in our own community."

Kat was lost. She had no idea what he was talking about, but didn't want to ask.

"They came in early morning. We didn't stand a chance." He looked at her. "I can't talk about it." He reached out and grabbed her wrist.

Kat fell, knees hitting soil. "Sui Duan!" she screamed.

Around her, people were yelling, running. They were all dressed in period clothes, as if two different films had collided into one another. There were people dressed like Sui Duan, Chinese men with their hair in braids, long tunics and soft pants. There were women too, but Kat could hear them more than she could see them. In the background, children cried. She did not know where she was. It was all mud and dirt and poorly built houses. People babbled Fookien and Mandarin and—she realized—broken Tagalog.

There were other people: guards in light blue uniforms with swords and guns, charging into houses, pulling out men and women and children, kicking at them, stomping on them and, at last, pulling the trigger. She recognized them as the civil guards from the Spanish colonial period.

And the stench. Everywhere, the smell of blood, of mud. Of people shitting as they breathed their last, of the fear that lingered as they were cut down, uncomprehending, defenseless.

*This can't be happening,* she thought. But then, so much had already happened.

"Sui Duan!"

Everything raged around her, a battle she did not understand. Kat got up and ran, weaving around bodies that fell. She sensed that no one could see her (she had seen enough movies with flashbacks in them to think so). A man fell in front of her. Kat screamed. His eyes flicked upwards, wide and scared, looking up at her. He screamed, the sound cut off by a soldier ramming his sword through the man's back. The word he yelled was in Mandarin, but Kat understood it enough. He had yelled *kwei*.

Ghost.

She heard Sui Duan's voice yell "stop" in broken Tagalog. A *guardia sibil* was dragging him out of the house. He was badly beaten, could barely stand. But still he fought, clawing at his assailant, trying to get back into the stone structure. There were people crying inside, the sound of a woman and the tiny high-pitched cry of a little girl. Kat ran towards Sui Duan. Rushing past the soldier, she knelt by him. All the doctor shows she watched cautioned her against touching an injured person, but she reached out and put a hand on his forehead. He opened his eyes.

"Kat."

Suddenly, Sui Duan sat up, catching the *guardia sibil* off guard. He pushed the man, grabbed his sword, and stabbed.

The *guardia* groaned then slid to the ground. Sui Duan was about to run into the house when another *guardia* caught him, pulling him by the hair.

"*Hijo de puta!*" he screamed, grabbing Sui Duan by the scalp and smashing his face into a nearby wall. Kat screamed, but the guard didn't hear her. He kept ramming Sui Duan's face in until his hand was coated in gore. He let the body drop, kicked it, and took out his sword.

"No!" Kat yelled.

The *guardia* was ready to stab Sui Duan. Kat ran, tackling the guardia. The man jumped, knocked aside by something he couldn't see. "*Myerde!*" he screamed.

Kat rushed to Sui Duan. She touched his forehead, her hand making contact with blood and—

*Is that his brain?*

AND THEN THEY were back in the school.

Kat was breathing heavily. She couldn't stop shaking. Sui Duan sat beside her, staring sullenly at a wall. Kat held up her hand. It was clean. *Did I really touch part of his brain?* She had so many questions, all of them jostling around in her mind, words that didn't make sense, not after what she had been made to see.

Night had fallen. She could see the headlights of her mother's car heading up the street. Sui Duan spoke.

"It was in 1603. Before this—" He waved his hand towards the school. "This was a Pariah, where all the Chinese were forced to stay. The government said we—the Sangleys, the Chinese—were plotting against them. That was their reason for what they did."

He spat.

"We were noodle vendors. All we wanted was a good life. We knew nothing about the government, nor did we care."

Sui Duan's image wavered. Kat realized that she was crying. She wiped hot tears from her eyes with the collar of her t-shirt.

"My family never had a chance," Sui Duan said. "But at least they died together. They were killed inside our house. And I—" he said, sighing, "I died on the spot where your locker is."

He sighed again.

"There. I said it. I died."

Kat reached out, took Sui Duan's hand. She was surprised when she made contact, his skin warm and soft. She imagined that if she felt for it, she would find a pulse on his wrist and his chest.

"You really care for your family, don't you?"

The question startled him. "Of course," he said. "Don't you?"

Kat was silent. Finally, she said, "It doesn't matter."

Sui Duan gave her a pitying look. "No family is perfect," he said. "But underneath all the cracks and crevices runs a foundation of love."

He smiled. "It took me decades to figure that out. Now the knowledge is yours."

"Why now?" she asked. "It's been centuries since you passed away."

Sui Duan stared at the street, at the incoming headlights. "It took me a while to realize what I had become," he said, "and even more time to realize that not everyone could see me, and that those who did had no interest in helping me. I had no living family to burn incense, pray for my soul, to send me off to heaven. I have waited so long, and when I saw that you could see me, I took the opportunity."

"But why can I see you? I've never been able to see ghosts."

Sui Duan looked at Kat. "I remind you of someone," he said, a smile playing at the corners of his mouth.

"But I've never seen you before!"

He shook his head, his grin getting wider, a secret he did not feel was his to divulge. "Time moves differently for spirits," he said, "but it is my familiarity that opened your senses to me."

Kat's eyes widened as she took in the possibilities.

Sui Duan saw her expression and laughed. "I'm not telling you." There were tears in his eyes.

"I don't know where your family is," she whispered, "but I think I know how I can help you find them."

She kissed his fingers, got up. "My mom's here," she said, "I'll see you tomorrow."

Kat gathered her things and went to the car.

WHEN SUI DUAN came to meet Kat the next day, she was smiling. "Meet me at my locker after volleyball practice," she said.

She could see him following her around, a shadow that darted in and out of her vision. It was comforting to know he was there, and strange to think that only a few days before, she had been telling him to leave her alone. *I wonder what kind of boyfriend he'd make?*

She laughed at the thought. He was old enough to be her great grandfather's grandfather!

He appeared again during Chinese class. Fortunately, *lao shi* was in a teaching mood and was discussing a story about a dog that spent all its life at the train station waiting for its master to come home. He waved at her. She smiled at him. *Lao shi* gave her an odd look, her eyes momentarily flicking towards the direction of Kat's smile. Kat raised her hand.

"*Lin Ping Ping?*" *Lao shi* said, addressing Kat by her Chinese name, as she did all her students.

"I don't know how to ask this in Mandarin," Kat said in Fookien, "but can you tell us about how the Chinese used to live in the Spanish times?"

*Lao shi* blinked, then smiled. "I'm glad you're taking an interest in our heritage," she said. "I'll read up on it and we can discuss that tomorrow."

Off to the side, Kat could see Sui Duan smile.

He was practically jumping up and down by the time they met after school. Volleyball practice went well, with the girls heading off for pizza. Kat elected to stay behind, telling them she was sitting this one out but would join them for the mall sale the next day. She changed outfits, making sure she was alone before sneaking back to her locker where Da Sin was already waiting.

"What took you so long?" he asked, then did a double take. "What are you wearing?"

Kat laughed. "Patience," she joked. She was in a white shirt, white pants, and white sneakers. Mourning clothes. She took out a large plastic bag. "I Googled this, but I'm not quite sure if I've got the sequence right."

She took out a couple of candles, lit them, and set them on the floor in front of her open locker. Then she took some incense sticks, secured their bottoms with lumps of clay, lit them with the candle flames and set them down as well.

"I hope it's the thought that counts."

Next came flowers, orange santans and red gumamelas picked from the school garden. She took out magazine cut-outs of a house, a car, some money (with dollar signs drawn on them in green crayon), and a dog.

"You've got to have stuff for the afterlife," she said, "This is Britney Spears' mansion. I hear it costs seventy million. This is Paris Hilton's Bentley, the one she didn't crash. I know you can't drive but I figure you'll be able to learn, wherever you're going." She held up the cash. "I don't know how to make hell notes. I hope they accept fake dollars." She was crying now, tears spilling down her cheeks as she chattered, laughing, trying to make light of what she was doing.

She put them all in a big can, lit a match and dropped it in, watched as the flames licked at the paper.

"What are you doing?" Sui Duan asked, even though he already knew.

"It's the only way for you to find your family," Kat said, "They died together. You went alone. You need someone who cares for you to send you on your way."

"Someone who cares for me," Sui Duan repeated.

Kat nodded. She took out cutouts of a man, a woman, a little girl, and a dog. "I don't know what your family looked like," she said, "Maybe you can imagine that this is them." She smiled, sucking in tears. "I even got you a dog. I hope you like Jack Russells. They're all the rage."

She took out a Bible, pages crumpled from use in religion class, opened it to a page she had marked with a Post-It. "I don't know what religion you practiced," she said, "But this might comfort you. I'm not very religious myself but—"

She began to read from the Twenty-Third Psalm. "Though I walk through the valley of the shadow of death, I will fear no evil, for Thou art with me..."

Through her tears, she could see Sui Duan growing faint. He was smiling at her, saying something that she couldn't quite make out. She leaned towards him, trying to listen to what he was saying.

"The light," he whispered, "It's beautiful."

She continued reading, "Thy rod and thy staff, they comfort me. Thou preparest a table before me in the presence of mine enemies."

The fire was dying down as the papers turned to ash. Da Sin had disappeared now, but Kat could still smell him, earth and blood, death and decay, the sickly odor that she had come to think of as his scent.

"Goodbye, my fold up boy," she whispered, "And good luck."

"Thank you, Kat," Sui Duan's voice whispered from far away, followed by a surprised "Mama? Papa?" Kat could hear footsteps echoing against a corridor, getting softer with each step, until they disappeared. The candles died, the scent was gone. Kat pulled her knees to her chest and cried.

LIFE WENT ON for Kat. Her parents eventually split up and she went to live with her mother. What surprised her was how okay she felt about it, how pleasant both her parents became when they could love her from their separate lives. She was nominated Captain Ball, led the school team to second place in the finals (the other team cheated), and just barely passed Chinese. It was easy to forget about Sui Duan most of the time, but sometimes, a shadow would dash across the corner of her vision, and sometimes, she would catch a whiff of what she could only describe as raw pork chop left out in the sun for a week.

And then there was the time she found a bouquet of santans and gumamelas inside her locker. Whenever these things happened, Kat would smile to herself. Wherever Da Sin was, she knew he was happy. And knowing that was enough to get her through the day.

MEGGY KAWSEK *graduated from Ateneo de Manila University with degrees in Information Design and Creative Writing. She's into too many things and has too many goals, but can never have too much tea. She organizes fun runs, draws comics, edits graphic novels, produces knick-knacks, and designs and animates stuff for a small company called by Implication. She will never give you up, let you down, turn around or desert you. She lives somewhere in Manila with the loins that bred her, over-achiever siblings, and a very black dog. She occasionally writes about things that should not be written about, but your mileage may vary.*

# The Tiger Lady

## Margaret Kawsek

IT IS IN the way she carries herself, or perhaps it is the tiger beside her, poised to leap at him. It is a massive animal, bigger than her, but she has it well under her control, with her right arm resting upon its back. The entire painting is a proclamation of her power: the young women that surround her are prostate, offerings of jade and peaches in their pink-tipped, delicate hands. The background is a mass of rolling hills surrounded by a gray fog that settle around her in curls. He is struck by her forwardness; her eyes are turned upwards, her chin down, her small, red lips curled in a knowing smile. *To seduce me,* the young man thinks, *or to kill me.*

He looks around and notices a spray of unfinished paintings. Young, naked men hastily pasted upon the other walls, some of them laid above stacked canvases just as hastily thrown atop each other. They look like him: tall, lean, and young; he wonders if he's come across any of them, or if, like him, they'd modeled for extra credit—but they are drawn exquisitely, with beautifully lined shoulders that abruptly end in undrawn limbs.

So unlike the tiger lady; she dominates the entire wall, overshadowing the beautiful male figures through sheer size and detail. His attention is fully on her again, and as he stares he feels her scan his nakedness. He grips the sides of the small, wooden bench provided for him to sit on, vainly shifting his body to hide from her gaze. He feels foolish for thinking that a woman in a painting is staring at him. Tearing away from her he tries to focus, instead, on the floors randomly strewn with old newspaper, and what looks to be huge, dark splashes of carelessly spilt ink.

The door to his left opens noisily. A woman's back is pressed against the old door. Her arms are full of paper rolls, jars, bottles and a large brush. They make clinking noises as she balances them. She shakes her head when he makes a motion to help her.

"Just sit there." Her voice is low and deep.

She twists to release the door and gracefully kicks it closed. She sets the jars and bottles on the floor a good distance in front of him. The rolls are thrown open like blankets. They curl in protest. Her hands sweep over them, pushing the continuous, persistent waves until the papers lay flat.

"Are you comfortable?"

It sounds like a well-rehearsed line. He shifts slightly on the bench, rubbing one foot on the other, wondering that himself. The air is too still. He finds himself counting his breaths.

"Just imagine I'm your mother, if it helps you."

He can see a slim figure underneath the cloth, knotted at her shoulder, as she adjusts herself.

His gaze travels to the movements of her clavicle, the rising and falling of her breath, and to her smooth, pale skin. He looks away when he realizes she knows he is looking at her.

"You don't remind me of my mother at all."

She snorts. He can't tell if she's amused or annoyed. She is fixing her inks, arranging them on the paper to force a stubborn curled corner down with their weight. She picks her colors carefully. Each time she does, she dips in a wet brush and squeezes the end. He feels a wave of heat rush down his body as he follows the way she gathers her fingers at the neck and pushes them down. The color spills from the tip and makes stains on the floor. He panics; he fights against the beginnings of desire lapping him down. He hears his own voice in his head cry: *control yourself,* and when he finds his bearing he asks her if they're going to start.

"I'm almost done preparing. The palette is good. Are you still cold?"

"I'm—" he pauses. "I'm okay," he lies.

"I'm going to sketch you now, before I apply the inks."

He straightens his back and tries to stay still. He feels the eyes of the tiger lady upon him again, and this time she is joined by the woman in front of him. He is not sure if she is real either. When he looks at her he finds her staring at the corners of his body, observing the creases, the dips, the arms. He's relieved to see that they are not judging eyes. They are wide, and deep, and lack the wrinkles he always expected from older women. She moves the charcoal in her hand, marking the paper, outlining his neck with her small, color-tinged hand. "I like your paintings." he says, in an attempt to break the silence.

"Which one?"

"The tiger lady."

"Xi Wang Mu."

"Sorry?"

"She's a Chinese legend. A goddess. My sister still teaches Chinese mythology, if I remember correctly."

"I don't think we've reached that far in class."

"I bet she did, and I bet you didn't listen. That's why she sent you."

Her entire arm moves with the charcoal in quick, calculated curves. He admires the way her body rocks back and forth as she traces and retraces the strokes. Her neck is stretched out, and the way the neck of her smock is being pulled by her movements exposes her breasts underneath. He is mesmerized, but the voice in his head repeats *control yourself*, and he diverts his eyes.

"Tell me about this exhibit. All of them are going to be men?"

"No, young men and her. Mostly her."

She points to the painting of the tiger lady.

"What did the tiger la—what did she do?" He turns his head towards the painting again. The woman shouts out, with definite outrage, "Don't move! I'm not done!"

He moves his neck back apologetically. The tiger lady is still watching him, and he feels her enjoy his powerlessness, his nakedness. "So what did she do?"

"She discovered the secret to eternal life through sex."

The word feels new, coming from the lips of a woman. He remembered when he would hear the word from his high school classmates in its most vulgar, as a taboo thing paired with adolescent teasing. The girls in the private school next door fumed and turned their noses away from the word, though some giggled shyly, but he had never heard any of them use it in a sentence. It had always been "that thing," or "you know," or "doing *it*." Nowadays his teachers and colleagues think of it as a scientific thing, always referred to as if it were a mechanical process: *reproduction, mating, coitus, engaging in intercourse.*

And now, *sex*. He swallows it. It feels raw in his throat and he spits it out. "Sex?"

"A boy. Sex. *Yin* and *Yang*, the balancing of the two between male and female."

She stops sketching. Her hand is coated in black powder. She gathers her hair at her nape and twists it, letting it rest on one shoulder. He spots a charcoal mark below her ear, and fights the urge to touch her. *Control yourself.* "How are you now?" She asks him, placing the charcoal back in the toolbox.

He feels a pressure around his waist. "Pretty warm, actually."

"Good. I'm going to start painting you now."

He expects her to reach towards the toolbox for a brush, but instead her hand searches her shoulder. She stops at a knot on her smock and undoes it.

For a moment he stops breathing. His eyes follow the path of the smock as it unravels: it is like water, and it touches points on her body briefly, brushing her skin. It tumbles forever, and when it finally lies on the ground he spots her feet inside the circle it forms. His eyes travel upward, to the length of her legs, to the gentle curve of her waist, to her erect nubs on her breasts, to her shoulders, to her neck, and to the face that is now looking at him without any shame or shyness. She is not smiling. She is not hiding. Her face is a patient, waiting beauty. He forgets her age. He forgets everything. He wills himself to look away—fighting the great urge to seize her—but he finds that he can't. Every inch of him wants to touch her. He trembles against the sheer force of his want, pushing against it. "What are you doing?" is all he manages to say, folding his hands over his erection.

"The paintings are all about *yang*," she explains. She kneels, gracefully, with her legs together as she bends down, and opens the toolbox, picking out a brush and shifting to a position on her hands and knees on top of the sketched image of him. "Particularly *yang* as sexual energy. "Particularly yang as sexual energy. I'm capturing a dynamic fire." She dabs color to his shoulders. It spreads quickly and she rushes to catch it with her brush at the corners of his limbs.

"I...this is..."

"Are you uncomfortable?"

"Yes," he says, too fast. "But...not in a bad way."

"It wouldn't be good for you to be too relaxed at this stage." She looks up from her position, glossing him over, and smirks—the first indication of a smile he's seen—at the seriousness of his face and the terror in his eyes. "Do you want me to give you something to make it less awkward for you?"

He is shaking. "I'll take anything."

She stretches upwards, letting her arms rise above her head and he marvels at the silhouette she forms. A toolbox near her is open and she takes out three small balls, each the size of a small piece of candy. "Take all three." He makes a motion to stand. "Wait. Don't get up."

*Oh holy Christ,* he thinks as she walks towards him. It takes three large steps to get to him. There is a small triangle of space between her thighs, and all he wants is to fill that space with himself, any part of himself. She signals for him not to move. She takes each pill and presses it to his lips. He briefly tastes her finger, briefly smells her scent while chewing the pills, each a spongy, earthy taste. Not unpleasant. He swallows them.

"She's also known for her daughters."

"Who?"

"Xi Wang Mu. Her daughters taught the Yellow Emperor the secrets. He talks about it in his book."

"*The Inner Canon.*"

Her eyebrows shoot up, but she doesn't look at him. His insides swell and he feels proud that he knows this piece of information, but at the moment his pride is disturbed; did his professor really describe him as a lazy, ignorant student? He remembers the moments she caught him sleeping in class, or not being able to recall the name of the Yellow Emperor, or the papers returned in a flurry of red marks.

He needed to appeal to her to let him pass, but she refused, citing the many chances he had, and the many instances where he ignored the opportunities to redeem himself. He called her names in his frustration; rude, loathing names, and this made her quiet. He expected a call for his suspension, but instead she gave him a time and a place, written on a piece of paper, instructions, and the words *Control yourself!*

"To always be young and healthy and balanced, and to control it through the energies that people don't even know they have... Xi Wang Mu used it to steal the souls of her young lovers."

Blood rushes through him, circulating faster. He feels his pulse quicken as he listens to her and he finds her voice beautiful. It is low and calm. She takes in small breaths between words. His body wants to cover itself in her breaths. He tries to move, to distract himself with the paintings on the walls but she clicks her tongue in disapproval, "I said don't move, I'm not done yet."

*Control yourself!* This time it is the professor reciting a mantra in his head. She is demanding his attention, repeating herself so he would listen: *Control yourself! Control yourself! Control yourself!* He is livid, and angry, and he hates lectures. He mutes her out as easily as he does in class.

"The exhibit is a balance," that artist continues. Her hair is falling across her face and he thinks it is unbearably beautiful. "Xi Wang Mu is at the center, and she is the vessel of *yin* energy. The surrounding *yang* energies must be enough to create a balance. How warm are you now?"

He finds himself breathing shallow breaths now, staring at her naked figure above his image, tracing him with a brush, her hands resting on the shoulder she had drawn. Somehow he feels the brush tracing him, activating his senses, spreading electricity from the points of contact. He feels her catch the sparks dancing across his body and create new sensations with each brush stroke.

*Control yourself!*

"How warm am I supposed to be?"

"Like fire."

"How will you know when I'm warm enough?"

Her eyes are upon him. She knows what he is trying to do. His heart stops at the knowledge of this, feeling fear more than anything, but the fire consumes his dread until he can't feel anything else except the heat on his waist and his desire for her. She walks towards him again and places her palm on his forehead, feeling for his temperature. She encircles him and he wills his breath to slow, realizing that his heart is pounding in his chest. "Can you show me how she did it?" he breathes.

There is a pause and the only sound he hears is his heartbeat. For a while he is ashamed of his request, and, muttering an apology, he straightens his back. He feels the tiger lady laughing at him now, and he imagines her voice in his head, *Can you control yourself?*

"Okay."

*Well, and how lucky you are, little boy.*

She takes his hand and leads him off the chair, where she gestures that he sit on the floor. "Is this your first time?" she asks. There is a silence, and sensing his hesitation she folds her hand into his. "It's fine."

She sits in front of him. "Water and fire. The energy that flows in you is yang, fast and uncontrollable. I am the water you must warm." She guides his hand towards her body and the rest of him is led forward. He is trapped in her gaze. She is poised, ready, knowing, and she reminds him of the lady with her hand resting upon the tiger's back.

"Come."

The voices in his head crumble easily under the order. He kisses her. He rushes to touch her and he cannot get enough. He runs his hands over her. He tastes her. He molds her and she moves with him, arching her back, bending her arms, twisting. It is a dance. "Let it control you," she teaches this patiently, repeating it as he discovers the crevices of her body. The raging burn overcomes him and it engulfs her with him. She tells him where to touch her, and for how long, and when to use his fingers. In turn she touches him and she tames his fire, keeping it from burning too fast, letting it settle only where she allows it.

She tells him that she is warm enough with the flush of her skin, so he plunges into her, and they rock together, fire and water melting and bending and creating sweat and steam. She is quiet; he only hears her small, calculated breaths, and when he groans she puts her fingers to his lips and makes him quiet, and this builds his energy and his desire even more and together they rock faster, as fast as his pulse, as fast as her breaths allow. Her eyes are open, focused, and he loses himself in them, the turbulent fire licking his insides, forcing itself out—

With a great, trembling cry he erupts inside her. He allows himself the pleasure of it. He is rigid, still, lost in her, and she is taking all of him. Jolts of fire rack his body, paralyzing him in the moment. "Thank you," she whispers. He feels the fire surge steadily from him. It goes on and on and she takes long, deep breaths, savoring it, smiling wildly as she absorbs him. When she is satisfied she rolls herself off and he wills himself to stop, but finds that he can't. His eyes tear open and to his horror the clear fluid turns to white, and then brown, and then a deep, dark red, and suddenly he is no longer feeling pleasure but a complete, searing, unimaginable pain.

"The aphrodisiacs work well. I didn't expect you to possess this much." She is watching him writhe on the floor. The tips of his fingers turn a deathly white. His eyes are wide open and all he can see is the painting with the lady and her tiger, both poised to jump at him, to strangle him, and she is laughing.

*Young men are always so willing to give their energy away.*

The fire eats him. It bites at his insides, stabbing repeatedly, and the agony of it makes him scream for anything to make it stop. But the woman stands, fingers his evidence on the floor, and walks slowly back to the blankets of paper. She smears it over his image and picks up her brush, watching him. The fire charges through his body one last time, eating the last, small traces of him, and with a burst of blood it leaves him, finally, truly spent and empty.

A gray fog creeps through the corners of his vision in soft, watery curls. The last thing he sees is the woman dipping her brush in his blood and spreading it like ink on his image.

CRYSTAL KOO *was born and raised in Manila and is currently working in Hong Kong. Her recent publications include stories in* The Other Room; Corvus Magazine; *and* Short, Fast, and Deadly. *She also has forthcoming publications in* First Stop Fiction *and* Philippine Speculative Fiction 7. *You can find her at http://swordskill. wordpress.com and @CrystalKoo.*

# The Perpetual Day

## Crystal Koo

THE STORY GOES that Jackson Chua, of Chua Drugstore: King of Pills, finally slept the sleep of the dead for the price of one carton of rat poison.

For days there was nothing else to say but: well, that marriage was going nowhere; he was nearly bankrupt anyway; he couldn't take any more of his mother's demands for a son. Shameless lies, especially the third because old Mrs. Chua was the type who played the bouzouki at a faux-Greek restaurant outside Binondo on Mondays and took hula hoop lessons on Saturdays, but everyone played along anyway.

Except young Mrs. Chua. She didn't let any of us see Jackson. At home, where the white, fluorescent lights and the laugh track from the TV noises frightened away the night, we imagined Miranda burning joss sticks and sobbing quietly at the wake in the funeral parlor, her dress whiter than cyanide salt, shamed for not having saved the marriage. We imagined her at the cathedral memorial service we hadn't been invited to, crossing herself and swallowing hymns, her dress grayer than arsenic, and keeping herself to the confessional.

Our eyes were red-rimmed. But not for the usual reason. Fear is stronger than death.

JACKSON WAS THE first one to succeed but he wasn't the first to try. That was Bonnie Ty, who had lain herself down the rails at Recto Station one night before. She didn't believe us when we reminded her the trains didn't run anymore because it was too dangerous to be on one. We brought her food and left her when she started flinging the styrofoam boxes at us. Her screaming was louder than the ringing in our ears.

We returned, exhausted, to Binondo's Kali-like arms and their arrays of abandoned scaffolding and small shops. We had done the search on foot with only the dim streetlamps on and it had been months since we had ventured into a lightless place so late in the evening. We clawed for the light switch, threw ourselves on the sofa, and turned the set on for the night.

Bonnie came back the next day and we pretended she had never left. No one wanted to talk about what it felt to be awake by yourself in the dark again.

We had always gone to Jackson's shop for our daily medication, which shows you how well it had been doing. After Jackson was buried, Miranda sold the drugstore for a very expensive song and took her daughters, moving out of Binondo and back with her parents in Greenhills. She never visited us again.

THE KOREAN BOY from the bakery—we kept forgetting his name because he didn't grow up in the local high school with us—made it on Sleep Watch before. He was supposed to be selling bean pastries with his aunt, but that summer morning he was a few hundred meters away from his father's bakery, resting against a utility pole, hiding his cigarette and watching Bonnie Ty wash her car. Above him was a man from the power company repairing the lines, suspended in the air in a plastic crow's nest.

This was during the early days, when people thought they were still sharp enough to operate machinery or be that high up in the sky. The poor boy broke the repairman's fall and nearly his own neck. The power company refused to pay for damages. His father found out about the cigarette. Bonnie Ty decided she didn't want to wash her car by herself anymore and hired an errand boy. Binondo was on Sleep Watch that night, with a camera zooming in on the shop's bean pastries for the opening sequence.

Nothing was good on TV anymore because nothing was on but Sleep Watch. Sleep Watch International was hit and miss because there's always something to criticize about a foreigner's house. Sleep Watch Local was just depressing unless it was about someone you knew who instantly turned into a minor celebrity. Nothing was good on TV anymore but we all watched anyway, cannibalizing other people's attempts to sleep, schadenfreuding on their failure. Otherwise we'd be like them, imagining our body growing roots down into the mattress, into the floor, into the soil, into the bedrock, which felt exactly like what we were lying on, bumpy and hard. Then we'd peel off our eye masks to another heart-stopping sunrise, grenadine red and tequila gold.

We had covered our mattresses with plastic and stored them behind our closets a long time ago. We had turned our bed frames into benches and low tables, more space for the snacks and board games that accompanied us and the people in Sleep Watch. We hoped one day somebody would suddenly find us lying face down on the sidewalk and would have the decency not to wake us up, but until then, Jackson's pills would have to do.

THE FIRST THREE weeks of the pandemic had been the worst. A week into it and the World Health Organization had declared it global and we felt better about having company but not nearly enough. When the sleeping tablets didn't work, we looked for painkillers, antidepressants, vitamins, ginseng, insulin shots, beta blockers, and diuretics, because the WHO didn't skimp on the list of sleep deprivation effects. Jackson made a small fortune.

Epifanio Ang held the nebulous record of being the closest to ever getting something resembling sleep and he did this by killing a cat and stuffing bits of it into steamed buns for dinner. He had always wanted to be on Sleep Watch and his stunt nearly got him there, if his son Leonardo hadn't stopped him after the first bite. The cat-killing cost Epifanio another piece of his sanity because he started having waking-dream hallucinations of the cat's ghost. But not his dignity, because anyone could have easily done the same thing for the two minutes of light dozing he claimed, even though all of us believed he had just shut his eyes and pretended so he wouldn't lose face in front of Leonardo.

Then Jackson Chua broke the record.

A WOMAN FROM the outside bought the drugstore from Miranda, which was bad enough. Her name was T.C., which was worse. We didn't know what it stood for. The identification she gave Miranda was printed with the same initials and showed a woman who had changed the name her own parents had blessed her with, possibly for colorful reasons. Ingrate. Harlot. Goose. T.C. Drugstore: Queen of Pills was not going to fly.

She wasn't planning to keep the drugstore. The shock reverberated among us like a pigeon smacking into one of the bells of our Basilica de San Lorenzo Ruiz, which brooded along with us. We called her bluff but it wasn't one. She didn't even hold a closing-down sale for the drugstore. She bought paint and new locks from Derek Tan's hardware store and hired a cheap contractor from outside to renovate the place.

We phoned Miranda.

"The Chua family's legacy," someone said.

"A historical institution," someone said.

"Jackson's memory," we all said.

Miranda must have cared very little for Jackson's memory because she said she couldn't do anything about it anymore.

T.C. WAS GOING to open a jazz club. It was going to be called The Jazz Club because there weren't any in Binondo. She said it would give us something to look forward to every night. She started posting ads for musicians in the jazz band.

In the movie version, the Korean boy from the bakery would join forces with her, another outsider, and dazzle the rest of us with his guitar skills and we'd finally remember his name.

But of course he didn't—he played the cello, not the guitar. More importantly he didn't even know such a thing was going on. Since the incident with the repairman, his father had him take breaks from work in his room in the small apartment above the bakery. The moaning from his cello reminded us of Jackson Chua and his carton of rat poison and we told ourselves we would never allow ourselves to be next.

We sent Leonardo Ang as an emissary. He told T.C. we were interested in buying the leftover stock from the drugstore.

"She said Jackson didn't leave any stock behind," said Leonardo. "She said there's nothing to sell."

"Bet she's keeping it all for herself," said Derek Tan.

"In the basement," Alan Lim added. "It's the only place big enough to fit everything Jackson had."

We tore her ads from our fences because bill posting was not allowed. Rafael See, who used to hold group drinking sessions with Bonnie in an attempt to black out, said T.C. stood for The Cunt and burned all her advertisements.

A WEEK INTO being deprived of Jackson's pills and we knew the ringing in our ears had leaped an octave higher. Alan Lim thought his legs were about to give way because his joints were so sore that he started looking for an electric wheelchair.

"She probably has Derek's biggest deadbolt installed in the basement," he said, waving a catalog that showed a wheelchair slim enough to fit him through the narrow corridors of his eatery's kitchen.

T.C. wanted musical instruments. We told Michael Sytengco that hiking up prices wouldn't work: he would have to chase T.C. out of his music store. Tell her you're closed, tell her everything's been bought, tell her you've run out of stock. Tell her the instruments she wants are locked in the basement for some mysterious reason. Sorry. Wishing you well. Love, Binondo.

Michael Sytengco had been bullied by Rafael See in high school and had never outgrown his paleness and his droopy eyes or his fear of doing a bad job of the operetta he had always wanted to write. The best he could do without falling apart when T.C. said she wanted a piano, a trumpet, a drum set, and a double bass was to give her the worst ones he had.

"And she couldn't tell how bad they were?" Leonardo asked.

"She almost stopped with the drum set. She looked at me for a few seconds," Michael faltered at the memory, "but she took it anyway."

We bought our medication in bulk from outside. There was never enough for our children, their children, our parents, their parents, somebody. All this work because T.C. bought the drugstore, because Jackson offed himself, because his marriage had turned sour, because business wasn't doing well, because he couldn't deal with his mother.

We felt better but not nearly enough.

"I NEVER ASKED for sons from Jackson and Miranda," said old Mrs. Chua one day on Sleep Watch International with a simultaneous feed on Sleep Watch Local. "His drugstore was doing well. He had a beautiful marriage." We turned off our televisions for a while after that interview.

Like with anything new, the Jazz Club had gotten into Bonnie Ty. Bonnie used to play the piano when she was a little girl with a weekly new pair of sandals that slipped off the pedals and spared us from hearing the wrong notes sustaining any longer down the street. She was now the pianist for The Jazz Club.

It was midday, lunchtime, with the kind of weather someone planning a garden wedding would want. A block away from Alan Lim's eatery, each beat T.C. played on the drums was clear and enunciated and her rolls gracefully covered Bonnie's clumsy transitions. It didn't sound like Michael Sytengco's worst drum set. The floor vibrated gently.

"I can't sleep," complained Epifanio Ang. He took off his hearing aids, which Leonardo tried to get him to put back on again but Epifanio waved him away and took a deep breath. It felt as if he was close enough to saying something about what Jackson did with the same problem and we felt a tremor in our bones. Someone started talking violently of the degenerating quality of the bean pastries at the bakery.

"I can't sleep," repeated Epifanio as though *we* were deaf and he tapped his feet against the floor. "That lady is playing too loudly. The cat is in her basement and it can't sleep either from all that noise."

He shot up from his seat like a jack-in-the-box and nearly knocked over the eatery stool. He forgot to put back his hearing aids. He went to Jackson's old drugstore and rang the bell. The drumming cut off immediately but Bonnie Ty went on for a few more bars. Some loud words. Some loud words repeated. We wondered if Epifanio would remember to ask her about the basement. Epifanio slamming the door.

"She will not stop the noise," he announced when he returned. "And she says there is no cat. But she will put an extra pillow in the bass drum and see if it helps."

The drumming returned, muted but still valiantly trying to cover Bonnie's wrong chords. We wished Bonnie had never returned from Recto Station. We sat watching the clock tick in front of us over our cooling casserole while Bonnie sped up and lagged and slipped off and crashed like a musical accident. They were trying to play something Nina Simone sang once, about dragonflies out in the sun and so on. Something that described the wedding weather we were in perfectly.

"Doesn't that song need a brass section?" someone remembered.

THE FIRST TIME we realized we couldn't sleep, we thought it was just us. So we went to work, went to school, left work early, didn't do homework because we were too tired. After the second night, we thought it was the summer weather getting too hot and we turned the air-conditioners all the way up and threw off our blankets. On the third night, we started taking pills and phoning each other at five in the morning and watching the sunrise together. After the fourth, we quit smoking and started changing diets and exercising and generating our own white noise in our bedrooms by setting our radio between stations.

Eventually we just turned the lights on. We might as well not be reminded of what we couldn't have.

DEREK TAN APPEARED in front of the door of old Mrs. Chua's apartment one night. He said it was okay if she believed what she wanted to believe about Jackson's death, he wasn't there to argue about that, but he wanted to ask if Jackson had left her any pills, any kind at all. The stuff from outside wasn't good enough. He wanted Jackson's pills. Did the rat poison come with complimentary pills?

Old Mrs. Chua said she never took any pills. They ruined her concentration when she was hooping, as if it wasn't bad enough she couldn't get any sleep.

Two days later, old Mrs. Chua moved out of Binondo, bouzouki and hoop, to live with her daughter's family. The apartment was put on the market and many of us pretended to be interested in it so we could open a cupboard and try to find an aluminum sheet of Jackson's pills.

THE FIRST SUICIDE happened in Panama. Most of us had been lining up in Jackson's drugstore with a list of what we needed when it came up on Sleep Watch International on the drugstore's TV. Jackson had been busy with the cashier and didn't even seem to have heard about the man who had jumped off the twelfth floor of a building.

After Jackson's death, the memory of that day frightened us, the rest of us who had watched the Panamanian's body hurtle down the air while Jackson rung up our purchases.

RAFAEL SEE SMASHED one of T.C.'s windows. He was trying to break into The Jazz Club and make for the basement. It was in the middle of the night and T.C., who lived in the apartment above The Jazz Club, ran down and found Rafael nursing a his bleeding hand outside the door. He was as plastered as a wine keg.

She got him a pad of clean gauze. She wasn't Pollyanna enough to invite him in but she sat on the curb, applying pressure on his bandage while he hummed that earwormy Nina Simone song of hers until Angela See came for him. Before they left, she told T.C., as a manner of thanking her, that her brother used to play the trumpet.

T.C. sent the Sees a bill for the window. Rafael put up a huge song and dance about her taking advantage of drunks but paid it anyway. We asked him what they talked about that night on the curb.

"Nothing," he answered. "She said people can start feeling sleepy after losing blood and asked me if it was working."

We had started avoiding Bonnie to make a point about her involvement with The Jazz Club but Bonnie Ty wasn't the type who noticed avoidance and sat on our tables anyway in Alan's eatery during teatime.

"She cooks really well, especially eggplants," said Bonnie. "She still owns a bed."

"What about the basement?" Leonardo asked.

"There's a very pretty staircase leading down to it. She painted it yellow and blue. Very Mediterranean."

"Have you asked about the medicine?" someone else asked.

"I told her all of you think she's keeping it for herself."

"What did you go and do that for?"

"She said it doesn't bother her what you think but she doesn't want to provoke you either by starting an argument."

"She's dangling a carrot in front of us. Where the hell are we supposed to get our stuff?" declared Derek Tan, who had bought a month's supply of muscle relaxants for the twitches in his arm that afternoon outside Binondo. "She keeps this up and we'll all end up like Jackson."

Bonnie was improving. Her piano still sounded like a colicky baby but it was growing up. One afternoon she and T.C. finished the song without making a single mistake. It happened to be luck—the colic returned the next time—but T.C.'s last shimmer on the cymbals in congratulations to Bonnie was so magnificent that Michael Sytengco forgot himself and applauded.

IT WAS LEONARDO Ang who had discovered Jackson. He had gone to the drugstore in the evening for some beta blockers for his father but no one was around. He called Jackson's cellphone and he heard it ring from the basement. It didn't stop. He went down the dusty staircase and found Jackson hunched over the granite-white, plastic folding table, his eyes closed and his head cradled in his arms, the way they used to pass the time in high school when the weather was balmy and the ceiling fan was lazy and the teacher wasn't worth listening to.

ALAN LIM ANNOUNCED that he had always been in love with Miranda (née) Go.

It wasn't that he was leaving his wife and kids for her that floored us but that he had to announce it. He called every one of us on the phone and made sure we all understood that Miranda Go had been God's gift to Binondo and he was going to bring her back.

That's why he had been Jackson's best customer.

We calmed him down. Miranda was no longer the ponytailed girl with the heartbreaking smile Jackson Chua had first brought to Binondo to meet his parents. Miranda was a widow whose husband had left her for something both of them had wanted.

We stopped him, if only for the sake of his family, but we couldn't stop Danielle refusing to sleep in the same bed as him. Sleep in the metaphorical sense, which was the only kind of sleep anyone was getting, but even that had gotten old and exhausting in recent memory.

"Wonder how she sleeps," said Rafael out loud, hooking his thumb out towards The Jazz Club, which he was strolling past, "metaphorically. She has a bed, doesn't she? Big enough for two?" Leonardo was with him and pretended not to have heard because he was discreet the way T.C. wasn't.

T.C. stuck her head out of the open window, the one Rafael had paid for, and said, "It's big enough for anything. Hi, Rafael." She asked him how his hand was doing and would he be interested in playing the trumpet with them. Rafael blustered and blushed and hid behind Leonardo.

Michael Sytengco was composing his operetta. When twilight fell and we renewed our nightly battle with the dark, the notes from his piano rippled against the fine grain of the timber of our homes, as clear as the stars we no longer wished to see.

LEONARDO'S HEART HAD spilled over, not because of the usual reason, but because he thought Jackson had beaten the night at its own game and so could the rest of us. He left him in the basement, deliberately quiet on the stairs, and went to the apartment above. Daisy had opened the door, her face and her limp pigtails sticky with tomato paste. She was sulking because her mother said it was Faye's turn to mix the spaghetti sauce.

Miranda was in the kitchen and Leonardo tried not to let the glowing ball of laughter in him overcome his words about the peace on Jackson's face.

IT WAS APPALLING, how good Rafael was on the trumpet. Even Michael Sytengco had to admit it. The notes were whiskey cascading over Bonnie's sharp rocks.

"So much for leopards and their spots," said Leonardo.

"A leopard's spots change when it matures from a kitten to an adult," said Angela See, who had been class valedictorian.

"My father isn't feeling well," said Leonardo.

It was the kind of thing no one gave an answer to because it would be too depressing but the tune coming from a few blocks away was so jaunty that Angela made an effort to make sure Leonardo didn't think she was being flippant. "No one is."

"He's nearly ninety. He can't hear a thing without his hearing aids."

The quiet ache of a minor seventh from the trumpet and T.C. followed Rafael's phrasing with a spontaneous, graceful rubato, slowing down time, speeding it up, stealing it for him.

"He watches Sleep Watch all the time. He's still obsessed about making it on that pointless program as if it's the only thing worth doing."

Angela didn't like where this was going. "I don't suppose he plays the double bass, does he?"

THE FOOTAGE FROM Sleep Watch International had gone like this. Shots of Jackson's store front, an aluminum roll-up gate, from different angles. Miranda in a paisley blouse and homely white shorts, glaring at the cameras, her nose red, cheeks creased, the flesh between her eyes wet. She hiccupped when she breathed. Her arms were stiffly crossed like dried, wooden stakes. Then she went in and locked the door. The reporter started to speak and they replayed their shots of the roll-up gate and Miranda, because that was all she ever let them see.

Old Mrs. Chua had gilded someone's palm and they got a coroner quickly, who declared Jackson dead by poisoning and no other questions asked. By the time Sleep Watch Local had gotten wind of what had happened and sent a crew, his body was already in the funeral parlor and his death certificate was being filed. Miranda would not let anyone in the reposing room. The funeral was a week later and by then Sleep Watch had lost interest.

Leonardo had been the only one outside of family Miranda had let in to see Jackson's body. The rest of us cowered in our living rooms, letting the glowing clips of Jackson's store front and Miranda's eyes reflect on our faces, knowing then, thinking then, hoping we would not be next.

IT WAS IN the morning, as the sky began to unfold itself to the light, when Leonardo rang up Sleep Watch. Epifanio had disappeared.

Leonardo had been watching one of their programs about a Swedish couple trying to go through one night with the lights turned off. He had gone to the bathroom when he noticed the door to his father's room open. The TV set was turned off. Epifanio had left his hearing aids on the armchair.

The crew from Sleep Watch Local came, with a whiff of instant coffee and the thought that this was a matter for the police, but there was nothing to film except Epifanio Ang's empty room and Leonardo saying his father has spent the evening before as usual drinking ginger tea and talking about the cat.

The rest of us searched the town for Epifanio and turned up with nothing.

"He's in her basement," insisted Derek Tan. "The cat's there."

"There's no cat," said Michael Sytengco, who had taken up a new habit of speaking audibly now.

"Why is she keeping that basement locked anyway?" said Alan, who was now living with his parents after Danielle threw him out of the apartment. He told her it wasn't him, it was the music that had stirred up those confusing emotions about Miranda. Danielle wouldn't have any of it. "Who is she to keep an old man and a cat apart?"

"Epifanio killed the cat," said Angela irritably, "because he couldn't sleep. It's the same reason why he's gone."

"Because the band's playing too loudly," someone said.

"Because there's medicine there she's not giving us."

"Because we're next."

Leonardo didn't say anything and gave none of us catharsis. Everyone went home with a headache on top of the usual migraine. Michael Sytengco didn't work on his operetta and the motor in Alan Lim's wheelchair broke down. The segment on Epifanio didn't air on Sleep Watch but we watched the channel the entire night anyway, feeding on other sleepless people in complicit silence.

LEONARD BRUSHED HIS teeth and gargled. It was seven o'clock in the evening. He hesitated at the sight of the striped pajamas. The last time he had put them on had nearly been a year.

Each button felt like a rung on a ladder leading to a cold abyss no one else knew about. If he dropped into the darkness, no one would notice. He would keep falling, the gravitational force pushing down his stomach until he went mad.

He turned the light off, the switch creaking its surprise. He almost cried out from the crushing embrace of the dark.

He had put the mattress on the floor in the middle of the room. Groping, he slipped under the starchy, newly-laundered covers and over the indentation he had left on the mattress before. He was suddenly claustrophobic and half-expected the walls of the bedroom to fall on top of him. He was sleepy—everyone was sleepy—but that meant nothing.

When he strapped the eye-mask on, he burst into a sweat. He lay there, frozen like a mummy, his arms forming a bridge over his stomach. He felt the pajamas sticking on his skin. He turned to lie on his side and thought how the movement meant he couldn't sleep. He gave a groan to fill his head with the sound, hoping it would chase out the thought. It was getting hotter and hotter under the covers and he could feel his pores oozing out sweat. The darkness was smothering him.

Jackson's face had been relaxed, oblivious to the poison that had killed him. His limbs had been loose. Leonardo tried to imitate him. He slackened his arms and legs and imagined his face was melting off. He imagined he was dead, dressed in his best suit in a casket, his head on a white, satin pillow and his fingers crossed together, everything under the glass, words of kindness pinned to the white, satin underbelly of the casket lid, everything was white and satin and so many flowers and so many faces.

It took a while for Leonardo to realize he was crying. The eye-mask was wet. His chest felt it was close to collapsing onto itself and he was about to fall off the bed. He pulled the mask off and sat up, trying to control his heavy breathing.

He didn't turn the light on. If he did, everything in its stark, normal whiteness would make him feel foolish for crying. The stark, normal whiteness had been there for so long it had already transformed the night into a perpetual day.

The apartment was on the sixth floor. His father's bedroom faced the main road and his own faced a smaller one. It would make less of a scene. He turned the air-conditioner off. The curtains felt almost like an accomplice, the way they slipped readily from his fingers.

The Jazz Club was across the other side of the road two blocks down. Practice was on and he could hear someone shouting very loudly. The voice was familiar, like the coldness of the thin, metal railing of his balcony. He leaned over. A small lizard clutched the edge with its toes, caught halfway between the careless slip of muscle and an angel's lofty hands.

THE STORY GOES that Epifanio Ang thought the cat was in the basement of The Jazz Club and the only way it would leave him alone was if he rescued it.

The rest of the story gets muddled. If you ask Angela See she'll tell you that despite what everyone is saying about the night Derek broke into The Jazz Club's basement, Rafael never knocked Epifanio down when the old man tried to force his way into The Jazz Club. Epifanio's boxer shorts were soiled and he looked like he hadn't eaten since he had left home; when he appeared at The Jazz Club's window and started rapping at the door, he'd already looked ready to faint. T.C. offered to bring him home but he kept insisting about the cat. He didn't have his hearing aids on and the argument escalated to the point that when Epifanio shoved T.C. out of the way, his blood pressure got the best of him and he fell down and the fact of the matter was Rafael had caught him.

Danielle still refuses to talk about Alan so there's no point asking her about his involvement in Derek's break-in. Distraction, says Bonnie. Alan was the distraction. There she was, practicing with Rafael and T.C., when Derek and Alan, who was back on his legs again because he didn't have another wheelchair, came in with the Korean boy from the pastry shop in tow. They said he played the cello. Close enough to the double bass. Not really, but T.C. sat Roh Sang-deuk behind the double bass anyway and the boy limply plucked the bass line to the Nina Simone song they had practiced before, missing notes. It was only when Epifanio came by and started losing it that Bonnie saw Alan moving to the basement staircase and she realized Derek was gone.

That everyone except Epifanio went down and found Derek with an open bag of tools and an even more open door to the basement is the clearest it's ever gotten to. Beyond that is the only thing that can shut Bonnie up. Alan and Derek don't even want to think about it. It's embarrassing to ask T.C. and Rafael's too distraught to talk of anything else but T.C. turning him down. The rest is all rumors about Jackson's ghost.

The bestsellers at Roh's Bakeshop are still the original green-bean pastries. Sometimes you can catch Sang-deuk's cello groaning away upstairs. He's the unlikeliest candidate, but if you ask Mr. Roh what his son saw in the basement, he'll try to tell you in his broken Tagalog the only thing Sang-deuk thought was worth noting about the basement was how dark it was before they turned the lights on. It was almost the deep, warm nothingness of sleep. Otherwise it was an ordinary basement, entirely empty except for a granite-white, plastic folding table starting to yellow on the side. The place was very clean. Almost shrine-like.

The turnout at The Jazz Club's mini-concert is a quarter of the town, including Alan and Derek. The bluesy, heart-wrenching wails Rafael pulls from the horn bring Michael Sytengco to tears and now everyone's uncomfortable. Leonardo has brought his father along. We should go say hi. They say Leonardo appeared at The Jazz Club, helping his father back on his feet, when everyone came up from the basement. What Leonardo was doing in his pajamas out in the street, his eyes red as blood, looking like Jackson's ghost depending on the light, but smiling, smiling almost like an idiot, squeezing the life out of his father, we never found out. There's a conversation starter and it'll last us a while, maybe even a month. Moon's full tonight. A quarter of the town is here and T.C. has just broken out the beer and who knows when the night is ending.

KENNETH YU *is a writer based in Quezon City, the Philippines, and is also the publisher/editor of* Philippine Genre Stories, *which has evolved from its original digest form in print, to an online fiction website at www.philippinegenrestories.com. His fiction has been published in various print and digital publications in his country as well as in North America.*

# Cricket

## Kenneth Yu

ABOUT *TAI-MAH*'S PORTRAIT rose tendrils of incense smoke, framing her visage in distinct waves of white curls. In their movement, they seemed more alive than the blank eyes and expression of the woman that the multiple red joss sticks had been lit for. They were much shorter now, having been burning for hours.

Unlike the smoke, the long lines of the family Chuang, extended family, and long-time friends and associates had long since dissipated. Everyone had made their obeisance, waved their sticks, and stuck them in the sand-filled pot. Everyone had caught up with each other, everyone's stories shared and told. The late, mid-afternoon lunch had been served—care of Lucy, from the heart of her domain, the kitchen—but dusk had fallen, and the leftover food turned cold, which brought the last set of straggling visitors to their feet and to their goodbyes. It was a Saturday, and one year to the day, by the count on the lunar calendar, since the matriarch of the clan had passed into heaven, her age a venerable one hundred eight, the most long-lived of a long-lived set of sisters—even if the last eighteen had been spent in a senile cloud that never cleared. Come the end of dusk, the house at last turned quiet except for the clink of china and silverware from the back kitchen, the distant sounds of residual dishwashing by the house help.

Richard, Lucy, and their son David had retreated to the second floor of *Tai-mah*'s house; the hosts were tired, and Richard grumbled all the way upstairs about the burden of being the youngest son, whose role and misfortune had been to care for such a long-lived mother, and whose responsibilities stretched so even after death. David, five and oblivious, played with a toy truck on the floor with his *yaya*. Lucy rested quietly on the couch, not even bothering to reach for the television remote control. She felt empty, and certainly did not have the energy to utter the words that would point out to her husband that she had played the role of host for the guests more, while he concentrated on his friends, brothers, and bottles of whiskey; that she had cooked and baked in the hot kitchen since early that morning while he slept; that while his brothers and sisters had indeed moved out years before, when they were all much younger, and he, the *sho-ti*, had been the one obliged to stay behind, he had been the one to inherit his mother's house—quite a large one. Now that she was gone, it was all theirs, even if it had taken one hundred and eight years for it to happen. They could sell it and move to a smaller, more manageable space, one they would own, she wanted to say, to leave behind all his complaints, and the weight of all her memories. But despite his misery, Richard never talked about moving, and so she left the words on her tongue, which became heavier with time passed and time still to come.

By nine-thirty that evening, everyone in the household lay in bed, even the house help; they had only bothered to watch one soap opera on the small TV provided for them in the back kitchen before turning in; they were that exhausted. The living room, which led to the dining area with a large lauriat table—beyond which were the sliding doors that, when open, extended to the veranda and a garden—lay quiet. This was where all the guests mingled, laughed, and talked; but now, the air hung still, as the joss sticks burned down, small, ember-red eyes glowing in the dark. Slowly, each one burned to a stub. When the last one winked out, dropping its ash-tip onto the pot's sand—when the last of the curls of incense smoke wafted up and vanished before the eyes on *Tai-mah*'s portrait, a black cricket chirped and made its way forward from behind the pot.

From what little filtered in from the outside, its carapace caught the light and reflected back a soft sheen. Moving forward, antennae trembling, it chirped once more, leaped forward, and landed on a high shelf with a photograph of *Tai-mah* when she was much younger; and then, after dropping its head in a bow, sighed, very much like a person in resignation of some daunting task.

RICHARD'S VOICE HALF-CAUGHT in his throat, which gave him a chance to change what he was about to say. Masking the many words he had intended with a cough, he instead only said, "Yes," and hastily took his cup and gulped several mouthfuls of coffee.

"Furthermore," said the cricket, in front of a seemingly stoic Lucy and a laughing, amused David, "you would do well to stop all your drinking, you and your brothers. I'm glad that none of you ever got into smoking. The smell! Heaven should be grateful for small blessings, few as they are."

The cricket had made its appearance at breakfast in the kitchen, dropping from somewhere above and startling the family. It had chirped its greeting: "Good morning." Lucy was the first to recover and greet it back—then, in a split second, blush at the absurdity of it all—but her embarrassment was immediately replaced with acceptance. David just smiled and clapped his hands. Richard took the longest to come to himself before unfurling the newspaper he crumpled in his hands. The cricket sniffed and addressed Richard immediately about his eating habits; before him was a plate of fried, fatty sausages and a double-heaping of rice, presenting itself like the evidence of a crime.

"This was prepared by Lucy!" Richard had replied, shifting the blame.

"Yes, every day," remarked the cricket, "on your instructions." A darkness touched Richard's heart at that moment, a fear he thought he had escaped, or at the very least, could ignore.

"And you," the cricket said to Lucy, no less firm, but with just a hint more kindness, "you may want to use that head of yours a bit more!" Lucy was taken aback, having expected some other kind of rebuke. In her mind lay the notion that she was the ideal wife, one that had existed for years even before her wedding. But for some reason, whether it was the timing of the cricket's words—that she was, for that morning, for that very moment, in the appropriate frame of mind and heart—or whether it was the way the cricket said it, she began to question where exactly she stood in the frame of her marriage. Instead of finding herself feeling any number of emotions that she otherwise could have expected, she instead found herself, strangely enough, uplifted with hope. Granted, it was only a small hope, less than a spark, but she liked it enough to consider ways to feed it.

The cricket turned to David.

"You are a happy one," it said. David, as if in agreement, laughed louder. "But isn't everyone, at your age?"

The cricket surprised them all when it took a long hop and landed on David's bare arm. It brushed its antennae gently on the young boy's skin. Up close, and given the insect's size—it easily covered half of David's forearm—it was quite fearsome-looking. Its mandibles were sharp, and its legs thorny stems that ended in clawed hooks. It was all angles, points, and sharp edges, and gave the impression that it was in a constant state of bristling. But where Lucy held her breath at how close it was to her son, and where Richard's hands tightened into fists and his body tensed in apprehension, David showed no fear, no sense of any danger. He just smiled at the cricket, and even dared to reach out and reciprocate by stroking with his fingers the length of its body. Lost in his touch was the natural roughness of a young child, replaced by what could have been affection.

"Hello," David said to it.

"Well!" the cricket replied. "Let's see how you all are, then." It hopped back onto the table, then off, and disappeared into the kitchen's darker recesses and crevices. For the rest of the morning, it popped up with its comments and complaints, to further surprise the family as they went about their business.

LUCY NEARLY DROPPED the lid of the wok she was cooking in when the cricket hopped from the floor to the table beside her hot stove. It remarked right away that it found her too sullen. "You are doing something you do well," it said. "And yet, you do not smile. Why do it, then?" It hopped away to perch on a ledge near the ceiling, overlooking the entire kitchen.

This time, Lucy found herself rising to the challenge of the cricket's question. She began moving with more vigor around the kitchen, actually banging her ladles and utensils against the wok, chopping food for lunch with vigor, stirring and frying with an energy she did not usually exert, cooking with insistence. What she was insisting on she did not know, but she acted in defense of herself, of who she was, and while doing so, she began, as the cricket commented, using her head.

She was not unintelligent; she had been near the top of her class when she was a student, though she did only a couple of year's work as a teller at a local bank before she married Richard. They met through their parents' mutual friend, and knew each other for nearly a year before the marriage had been set, agreed upon by both of them and their parents. It seemed so natural. She was no great beauty, and her family was not rich, so she knew her prospects were narrow. Richard seemed like a nice enough man, six years her senior, though she did not like the way he scratched himself in places when he thought no one was looking, or the way she caught him slipping off his shoes under the dinner table to curl his toes. He said the right things, to her parents as well as to her. The issue of him being the youngest in a family of six boys and five girls came up only once, but her parents, particularly her mother, brushed it aside as unimportant. She had not known what to think of marrying a youngest son, and so thought nothing of it herself, until the days after her wedding stretched into the weeks, months, and years of being anchored to a filial duty that her husband resented, and infected her with. Looking back now, it had not been so bad after all; she learned to cook from her mother-in-law, and became as good, if not better, than her. When the older woman became too old to cook, the kitchen became hers.

Became hers, she realized. For the first time in a long time, she smelled the spices from the steaming food in front of her, tasted their sharp tangs, and broke into a smile that took years of lines and inherited bitterness from her face.

DAVID SAT ON the living room floor alternately reading his picture books and playing with scattered toys. When his *yaya* saw that he was behaving, she left him to help outside in the garden with hooking the laundry onto the clothesline, still within sight of him but separated by some distance and the sliding glass-paneled doors. The cricket made itself visible across the floor from him; he smiled at it but did not move toward it. Instead, David picked up a book and read aloud from it, as if to no one in particular but really intending for the cricket to hear his words. The insect inched closer and closer, and when it was near, David allowed it to perch itself on top of his shoulder. He finished the book, and another. By the end of the fifth book, the cricket found itself on the coffee table, on a level with David's eyes. They regarded each other quietly. They did not need to exchange any words. The cricket watched David, aware of his youth, and to its eyes he seemed like a clean blank sheet of paper on which anything could be drawn or written.

Since breakfast, Richard had moved restlessly around the house. He could not stay still, moving from the ground floor to the second and back down again, consciously wandering between rooms and sections of the house that were empty. He avoided the kitchen, knowing his wife was there; he did the same for outdoors, where the house help was busy; several times he passed his son sitting on the living room floor, engrossed in his books and toys, and paid him no mind.

The feeling of dread had magnified since the cricket's first appearance. He could not lay a finger on or say clearly what he feared, but he sensed some impending trepidation, a moment of reckoning that he had to face, and he knew he was not ready and would most certainly be found wanting. As to why, he could not say. But he blamed the cricket.

Eventually, he chose his sanctuary in the small, corner stockroom he converted many years ago into a home-office. He would normally never enter this room on a Sunday, but today he found himself walking into it. He shut the door behind him and sat at his desk, settling into an old, fraying, office chair. The desk was covered in old receipts and invoices, correspondence, and office bric-a-brac that had piled up over time. Many of the documents were on matters that were long overdue for his attention, which he procrastinated on, and did not even glance at. Instead, he sat back, put his hands behind his head, closed his eyes, and resolved to forget the morning and the cricket through an activity he often engaged himself in: self-pity.

He thought about money, how little he had and how dependent he was on the salary he was given from the family business, run by his *Ahiya*—his eldest brother—and his wife, who controlled its finances. How all his other brothers seemed to be doing better, whether with their own professions or their private, family lives. How they all seemed to be able to travel and go to different places as they pleased, while he had to wait to be invited so that he could share rooms and meals and other accommodations to fit his shoe-string budget. How his sisters seemed to have married into what they wanted, for the most part, but really, their lives did not matter so much to him as his brothers', in comparison. He laughed and put up a front when he was before them, of course—nothing was wrong, everything was all right, I'm doing fine, I can handle this. All his worries he would never admit to anyone, but he blamed the secret unfairness of it all on his being the youngest in the family, neither for the first time, nor the last. Why must the burden of being left behind to care for the aging parents always fall on him? He let the self-pity wash over him, mixing it with the images of his brothers in their own homes, his sisters with their husbands, and the pity and scorn he believed he saw in their eyes, and yes, even in their children's eyes, whenever they saw him. There was no respect there, he was certain of it, even when they greeted him with smiles and hugs.

What had his *Achi*, his eldest sister, once said about him? That he was the slowest and most dim-witted of them all.

The duty of tutoring all of them through school fell to his eldest sister, and he recalled how strict she was with all of them. She expected nothing but good grades, saying how important it was for their future, but it was with a forlorn expression that he would often watch his other siblings leave the study table ahead of him, yes, even his youngest sister, the flighty, bubble-headed one who had gone against her father, shunned the Chinese-Filipino he asked her to meet, and instead married a Swiss-Canadian; even she seemed to be better off in Canada, a first-world country. It was so unfair that many of his siblings needed so little effort to pass their exams while he would spend hours, hungry and past dinner, studying and memorizing, only to do poorly on his tests. *Achi* shouted and scolded and put up her hands in exasperation, and come high school he finally shouted back. She left him then to his own devices, and it took him five years to pass high school instead of four, and a bit longer to get through college. But he got through! Yet, it seemed as nothing compared to how everyone else had done. *Achi.* She was a successful accountant, and the way she remained distant from him ever since he broke off from her stood out in stark contrast to the way she comported herself with the others.

"Perhaps," the cricket chirped from an upper shelf where boxes of old car parts had been stored, "you would be better off humbling yourself instead of presenting yourself so highly."

Richard opened his eyes, found the insect, and glared at it. "What would you know?"

"Enough. Much. Too much," the cricket said. "Even you must admit that for all your posturing, your siblings know the truth."

"How could you know?" Richard said. He felt his blood rising to his face.

The cricket ignored the question. "Many of your brothers are the same as you. They are not the same as their outward appearances of success. Behind their public faces, they have great failings in their homes. You may draw consolation from this, but in truth, it is a tragedy, because you, your family, are all the same.

"Why not humble yourself?" the cricket repeated. "For your sake. For your wife's. For your son. Never mind your siblings, for now, but you would be much happier for it."

"You leave my son out of this!"

"He is a good boy. He could be successful, in the right way. Don't infect him with your bitterness!"

Richard could no longer control himself. He felt his rage rise at the insolence of the insect which dared to speak to him in this manner. He reached for the nearest object—a mug used as a pen holder—stood up in a rush, which sent his chair crashing against the wall, and threw the mug at the cricket with all his might.

His aim was off and the mug crashed and broke into many pieces just to the right of its target. An explosion of pens and white ceramic burst and fell to the floor. The cricket jumped and fled, squeezing through a small hole in the upper corner of the doorway and out into the main portion of the house.

Richard flung the door open and gave chase, brandishing one of his slippers. He limped quickly after the cricket, one foot unshod, swinging his arm at the cricket in wild, violent arcs and screaming invectives at it. The cricket flew fast to the left, to the right, avoiding Richard, leaping and flying as fast as it could for dear life. Richard, throwing all caution away, went after it, hitting and bumping his body against furniture and shelves, toppling them over and sending picture frames, vases, books, and appliances crashing to the marble floor.

The noise brought Lucy from the kitchen, her mouth agape in shock and fear. She ran for her husband to try and hold him back, but when she saw him follow the cricket into the living room, taking a swing that dealt a glancing blow to David's forehead, she forgot everything else and gathered her wailing son into her arms and carried him to the corner of the room, shielding him with her body.

All the doors and windows were closed; there was nowhere for the cricket to run. It flew as high as it could, from one upper corner to another, but Richard's rage fueled him and gave him strength beyond what energy the insect could maintain in escape. It flew much more slowly, and much lower, leapt in slower flight, until, with a mighty swing, Richard connected at last with a satisfying thwack, sending the cricket smashing against the wall. It fell to the ground, and Richard was upon it, bringing his slipper down on it again and again, shouting incoherently all throughout until he could no longer lift his arms and needed to stop, to at last draw in great deep breaths for his tired body. The cricket lay at his feet, a mess of yellowish-green viscous fluid mixed with the smashed mess of its crushed body.

"What did you do?" Lucy screamed, cradling David's head against her chest. "Why did you kill it?" The bump on David's forehead was turning into an angry red. He struggled hysterically against his mother, reaching out with his hands and arms for the cricket; it was all she could do to hold him.

"Shut up!" Richard shouted back. "Just…shut up! And shut him up, too!"

"Why did you kill it?" she repeated. "David liked the cricket! We could have kept it for him!"

Richard did not immediately answer. Instead, he turned away. The anger, spent like a volcanic eruption, was leaving him. He felt drained of energy, but not of the dread and fear. No, those remained, like a loaded gun still aimed and readied against his chest. He could not explain what he did, or why. But his pride and bitterness—and yes, his self-pity—those he did not even try to push away.

"He'll get over it," Richard said to Lucy, and he put all the cold arrogance he could muster into his words.

Something hit him on his head. It hurt, but only slightly, not enough to cause him to even shout out. He turned and saw his son standing defiantly up against him, one foot also unshod, his face a mask of hatred and anger. The slipper he had thrown at his father lay on the floor and to the side after having bounced off Richard's head.

Richard stared at the thrown slipper, then at his son, and then he could only stumble in a daze back to his home-office. The dread and fear inside him increased with each step, and even when he closed the door behind him, he knew that it would not be enough to keep his tragedy away.

*Born in 1982,* **DOUGLAS CANDANO** *holds a BA in Develop-*
*ment Studies from the Ateneo de Manila University*
*(Development Studies Departmental Award, Loyola*
*Schools Awards for the Arts in Fiction), and a Masters of*
*Urban Planning degree from McGill University. He has*
*received a Philippines Free Press Literary Award and a*
*Don Carlos Memorial Award for Literature for his short*
*stories, and has received fellowships to the 8th Ateneo*
*Heights, 4th Ateneo, 45th Dumaguete, 7th IYAS and 14th*
*Iligan National Writers Workshops. His stories have ap-*
*peared in* Heights, Story Philippines, *the* Sunday Times
Magazine, *the* Philippines Free Press, *the* Philippines
Graphic, *and the* Likhaan Journal of Contemporary
Philippine Literature, *and have been anthologized in*
Philippine Speculative Fiction, Volume 1 *(2005) and*
A Different Voice: Fiction by Young Filipino Writers
*(2007). He is currently working on his first collection of*
*stories.*

# The Way of Those Who Stayed Behind

## Douglas Candano

LAST YEAR, AS you may remember, I was unable to go to Edmonton for the annual CIPA conference due to the abrupt death of my great-grandmother. I never would have imagined that my first trip back to Manila would be for a funeral, especially after having been gone for so long. I also didn't expect that I would be going back alone, since I had been meaning to schedule a family vacation to the Philippines over the past couple of years.

In some ways, though, I was relieved that Miriam had an urgent board meeting on her pet project and that the kids were in the middle of their finals. Although I would have wanted the kids to meet their relatives, I was a bit hesitant to have them accompany me on this trip. Since a lot of changes have surely happened over the years, I certainly didn't want to disappoint them at how different Manila was from all the stories that I had told them. Besides, their presence would have hindered me from making an inventory of family assets—something that occurred to me once the initial shock at hearing about *tai ma*'s death had worn off. I guess all the horror stories about family members suing each other must have gotten to me, and I figured that it would be in the best interest of my family to know and protect our entitlements, especially with both my parents dead for over twenty years.

And so, shortly after the funeral and a couple of days before my flight back, I visited the old family compound in Pasay. To nip any suspicions about my visit to what I heard was an otherwise idle property that had been unofficially turned into a storehouse even while *tai ma* was still alive, I had told my Grand Uncle Victor that I wanted to look for some old personal items to ship back to Vancouver.

I was nervous as the car made its way through the almost unbearably dirty and cramped side streets of Pasay. Although I was going back to the scene of some of my more memorable childhood memories, I felt like I was going to an unfamiliar, potentially inhospitable place. Save for my belief that I would be able to find the documents I needed, I hardly knew what to expect.

All these inutile, meandering thoughts disappeared as the driver stopped at a familiar, tall, brown gate. After a few moments, a shabbily dressed guard drew open the gates to a driveway that I haven't seen since I lived in the compound.

It had been nearly two decades since the abduction of my cousin Raul brought to a close that month that had already seen the high-profile death of Charlene Mayne Sy during a botched rescue attempt. And, while Raul was released unharmed after a couple of days (and around $15,000), the shock of the whole incident prompted Miriam and me to seriously consider starting our family in a less hostile environment. Canada had just relaxed its immigration policies a couple of years before and quickly made its way to the top of our options. Surprisingly, our idea was well received by the family, with *tai ma* even saying that it was a golden opportunity for childless newlyweds still searching for their way in life. Consequently, by the middle of the following month, we arrived in Vancouver, where we eventually gained citizenship, had children, and made a name for ourselves in our respective fields. In the same way that Miriam worked herself up the corporate ladder from secretary to executive, the post-graduate degree that I pursued upon reaching Canada eventually led to my present post as an adjunct professor of Political Anthropology.

I was still thinking about these life changes as I stepped out of the car and onto the sloping driveway of the main house. Looking around, I could see that the compound had also changed over the years. Aside from an apparent need for immediate renovation, the buildings seemed smaller and more crowded, while the garden playground where my cousins and I used to play had fallen into the trappings of disuse, with its slides and swings rusted and bent beyond normal repair. Perhaps the most noticeable change was the presence of what appeared to be a small, brightly painted Chinese temple in the deepest area of the compound, right on the spot where my Aunt Raquel's (Raul's mother) house should have stood. A concrete wall with a small gate was now located on the path that had led to Aunt Raquel's house.

The new structure made me uncomfortable. While the funeral had some of the usual Chinese rituals such as the burning of the paper house, money and cars, and the placing of chicken's blood on *tai ma*'s portrait, all this had occurred after the requiem mass. As far as I knew, we had all been raised as Catholics. Even *tai ma* had been baptized, although I must admit that I remember her seemingly making small paper birds fly by chanting what sounded like gibberish, aside from spending hours staring at a porcelain bowl filled with water.

I was so preoccupied with the small temple that I was startled by a voice that said the family would regularly pray there on Sundays. Turning around, I found myself in front of a non-descript, middle-aged man who introduced himself as the caretaker.

After mentioning that Grand Uncle Victor had called him about my visit, the caretaker said that he had been surprised when he learned about my existence because he thought that he had met the whole family throughout his decade of employment. Although I found his statement odd since it was hardly plausible that I was never mentioned in ten years, I decided that it barely warranted a response. However, as he fumbled with the keys, I asked him when the last members of the family had left the compound.

The caretaker replied that Grand Uncle Victor's family had moved out sometime during the previous year, a few months before the sudden decline of *tai ma*'s health. He added that while *tai ma*'s age had always been a cause for concern, her abrupt illness and death had caught them all by surprise. Finally finding the right key and opening the door, the caretaker wondered aloud what he and the other members of the household help would do now that the family matriarch had passed away.

I kept silent as I entered. I didn't know what to say, and felt that my transient status hardly gave me the authority to speak on such matters. Aside from this, I was bothered by the caretaker's use of the Chinese word for matriarch when he referred to *tai ma*. Although we had never called her that, I had heard it used a few times by my relatives during the wake and funeral —something that I just thought to be some sort of new convention.

My silence probably made the caretaker realize that I wasn't there to fraternize with him, since he excused himself after a few moments.

As I walked around, I noticed that things were actually better than what I had expected. True, the house was a bit dusty and some of the rooms were filled with boxes and scattered medical equipment, old appliances and various knick knacks, but its main areas were generally clean. It was clear that *tai ma* had given permission for the rest of the family to store their belongings in some of the infrequently used rooms. In this sense, the layout had been mostly unchanged, as I noted as I made my way past the plaques and trophies that were still displayed in the small anteroom and through the living room with its clunky big screen TV and huge vases, while sneaking a peek at the dining room before moving up the stairs to the more private areas of the house.

The first thing I noticed when I went up to the second floor was that the bookcases were still in the corner of the main corridor, all of them full of crumbling volumes and ledgers that were propped up by a couple dozen bookends. As you probably expect, I felt compelled to take a look although I was certain that they contained none of the documents I hoped to find. I knew that I was alone and since time was hardly a concern, I could even browse through some of the Chinese texts if I wished.

I went through the contents of the bookshelves methodically. Although the books had always appeared haphazardly and asymmetrically ordered, with some even placed with their spines towards the insides of the shelves, it soon became apparent that someone had put a lot of time and effort in thematically organizing the bookshelves. I guess this explained the numerous bookends and why some of the shelves were only half full. Reading materials on history were divided by subsections relating to time and location, while production books were ordered according to each production phase. Since everything was ordered in such a coherent manner, I was a bit taken aback when I saw a small, handbound volume with a crude drawing of a man seated in a lotus position wedged in between a couple of stained Fujianese cookbooks.

I was immediately drawn to the book, which bore, in bold Chinese characters, the title *The Righteous Way of Heaven in Tumultuous Times.* Looking at the inside cover, I became even more excited when I read that it was produced in 1989 by The Righteous Way of the Loyal Children of Heaven Society.

During my first few years in Vancouver, I would hear rumors within the Chinese-Filipino community about the resurgence of several groups in Manila that claimed to be the successors of old Mainland secret sects such as the White Lotus Society and the Heaven and Earth Society. The rumors had it that at the height of the kidnapping terror, when armed bodyguards had proven themselves useless, and people started to realize that avoiding public places was of no deterrent, the teachings of these groups played a part in strangely aborted abduction attempts. There was talk about a family pre-empting a kidnapping by using what was called a karma mirror, while it was also said that another family had spontaneously brought back a kidnapped son by moving a small effigy of the boy along a table. Even stranger was the talk about would-be kidnappers being attacked by little paper figures before they could complete their plans.

With these thoughts still lingering in my mind, I began to leaf through the book, even before I sat down on the chair at the far corner of the corridor. Despite my less-than-stellar grasp of written Chinese, I was surprised at the speed and ease at which I went through the text. It was as if I instantly recognized and understood every character, which gave me the freedom to occasionally reflect as I read.

The book began with the near-death experience of Jade, a Fujianese village girl, who, upon regaining consciousness, finds herself in a vast palace where the ground is made out of gold and where there appears to be an infinite variety of pavilions, halls, and terraces bordered by clear streams and pools. Although amazed by her otherworldly surroundings, Jade is unable to explore the palace since right in front of her is an immense golden lotus, where an extraordinarily tall old woman with a kind, sad face is seated in the middle.

At this point the text shifted into verse as the old woman introduces herself as the Eternal Venerable Mother, who had given birth to the first man and woman and had sent mankind to populate the Eastern world. There, her children have lost their original nature as they learned to immerse themselves in vanity and avarice. This has been a cause of great suffering for the Eternal Venerable Mother, whose weeping and imploring letters have gone unheeded.

The prose portion of the text then resumed, with the Eternal Venerable Mother telling Jade that she has wanted nothing more than for her children to return to their native land in the Original Home in the World of True Emptiness and be reunited with her on the golden lotus throne. Despite her unnoticed tears and the underwhelming response to her pleas, she has always been hopeful that this reunion will take place. This hope has led her to send messengers to reign and preach the true dharma throughout the three kalpas, or stages of time. The first messenger was the Lamp-lighting Buddha, who reigned from a five-leafed azure lotus throne throughout his kalpa, which lasted for 108,000 years. He was then followed by Sakyamuni Buddha, the present messenger, who sits on a seven-leafed red lotus throne. While the first two messengers have brought about the repentance of some, the vast majority of people continued to live in sin as the true dharma has gradually given way to the false dharma. This meant that the present kalpa was about to end. The 27,000-year reign of Sakyamuni Buddha would soon be over, and the Maitreya Buddha, the final messenger, will arrive to begin his time on the nine-leafed white lotus throne.

The Eternal Venerable Mother then tells Jade why she has been summoned to the golden lotus throne. As in the past, the turning of the kalpa will bring forth death and chaos as the present world order is destroyed by successive waves of calamities. Because only the followers of the true dharma will be able to live and prosper during these times, it is imperative that people prepare for the coming of the Maitreya. According to the Eternal Venerable Mother, the quality of Jade's accumulated merit has placed her under the divine grace of heaven. Consequently, she has been chosen to oversee the preparations for the Maitreya's arrival.

The Eternal Venerable Mother then asks Jade if she wished to accept this responsibility. Jade agrees without hesitation, and the Eternal Venerable Mother proceeds to teach her the secrets to the salvation of mankind. These secrets formed the basis of The Righteous Way of the Loyal Children of Heaven Society, which was founded by Jade when she returned to earth and adopted the title of Grand Matriarch of the Righteous Way, which has since been handed down to the eldest daughter in each generation of her descendants.

Although I should have hardly been surprised by this hereditary title, it was suspicious to read it in the book after hearing a shorter version of it used to refer to *tai ma* over the past few days. As much as I knew that it would be premature to make any definite conclusions, it was hard not to connect the title with the things that I have encountered.

These things were not only limited to my experiences during this trip. Aside from the presence of the temple and the fact that such a book had been hidden inside the house, I couldn't help but remember what *tai ma* was like. While she certainly had her warm moments, she sometimes carried herself with an air of aloofness that I had always attributed to the language barrier. She seemed to place importance in setting aside a few hours of the day for herself. When my mom was still alive, she would scold me for sneaking into *tai ma*'s room, where there was always a stash of assorted cookies, during these quiet afternoons. Although I quickly learned to avoid *tai ma*'s room during those times,

I remember catching brief glances of her making her little flying birds of paper, or seeing her place burned scraps of paper in bottles of water to make the Chinese medicine that would be given to us whenever we got sick. We never really knew if the medicine was effective since it was always given to us to drink when we were at the tail end of our antibiotic cycle. However, I was intrigued by the flying paper birds, which I never really understood since my attempts to bring them up with *tai ma* were constantly met with harsh chastisement—something that caused me to think that it was always her time of the month, although she was probably a couple of decades into her menopause then.

It was difficult to think about all this. As ludicrous as it was to consider that my family was somehow involved in The Righteous Way of the Loyal Children of Heaven Society, or had perhaps, even founded and propagated the sect over generations, I could not help but dwell on the possibilities. If there was some kind of involvement, then not only was *tai ma* concealing the truth from me all these years, but the other members of the family had also been aware of the sect and had perhaps even participated in its activities. What else could have reasonably explained the presence of the temple? Despite *tai ma*'s clout, I doubt that Aunt Raquel would've readily agreed to have the house that she had inherited replaced by such a structure if she didn't approve of it. It was also impossible for anyone in the family to not know about the temple once it had been constructed. Besides, the caretaker did say that they worshipped there every Sunday.

I tried to keep these thoughts in check before they could get any more complicated. I knew that my long absence had hampered my ability to understand the situation in Manila, and that there were other explanations aside from my deliberate exclusion from such an important family matter. Besides, there were too many fundamental things that I didn't know, the most important, perhaps, being actual information about the sect. Save for that pseudohistorical origin story, I knew nothing about the beliefs and activities of the Righteous Way of the Loyal Children of Heaven Society. This made it hard to prove any relationship between the sect and my family, despite the link that I suspected. Even *tai ma*'s actions did not mean anything, however weird they may have been.

Without anyone to talk to, I knew that I could only find the answers I sought in the book. Immersing myself in the next few pages, I gradually noticed that the next nine short chapters were written using the same basic formula.

Following the prose-verse-prose structure of the origin story, each of the nine chapters focused on the Maitreya Buddha's messages to specific groups of people who will become gravely affected by the turning of the kalpa.

Each of the chapters began with the Maitreya opening the Book of Heaven to look at the state of the world. In what was probably a good indication of the sect's intended audience, the Maitreya's attention was curiously limited to the spread of the false dharma in the Philippines during the early 1990s, with the Book of Heaven showing the misdeeds of each group of people destined to suffer the most at the end of the present kalpa.

After the Maitreya recites a litany of sins attributable to each group, the way towards redemption would then be explained in what I understood to be the sect's basic teachings. Aside from the obvious demand to cease these immoral activities, the Maitreya also called for abstinence from meat, gambling, and alcohol. The Righteous Way also involved the strengthening of the mind and body by the cultivation of *chi* through meditation and exercise. While the physical exercises were only discussed in general terms throughout the nine chapters, meditation was sometimes mentioned with the memorization of what was called the

*Wordless True Sutra.* This was composed of eight characters that translate as "Eternal Venerable Mother in Our Original Home in the World of True Emptiness." Salvation would be achieved through the regular chanting of this sutra and the faithful observance of the Righteous Way, which would enable a repentant sinner to gain enough merit for a place within the protective walls of Cloud City when the kalpa ends.

In contrast, the rejection of the Righteous Way would have dire consequences as non-believers would suffer, starting from the string of calamities that herald the turning of the kalpa. These initial calamities were alluded to in some chapters as "the darkness and gunfire amid the loosening of the earth and the storm of flames"—a phrase that was especially chilling for someone who lived in the Philippines during the early 1990s. This made it even more difficult to comprehend the scale and scope of the suffering that will supposedly be sent by the Eternal Venerable Mother as mankind's final punishment for refusing salvation.

According to the book, the final punishment of those who reject the Righteous Way will begin when the true dharma is finally extinguished. Shortly after all the true scriptures vanish from the world, the course of the sun and moon will be altered and the climate will change abruptly. This cosmic imbalance will be followed by extreme calamities as earth, wind, fire and water are thrown into chaos, destroying all crops and leaving scores of corpses to rot. A black wind will then blow through the world to reduce all surviving non-believers into piles of white bones and pools of blood.

The mass holocaust of non-believers and the destruction of the world was apparently only the first part of the turning of the kalpa. Some of the chapters made references to the afterlife, describing the serpentine queues that would stretch through the many halls of King Yama's palace. There, sinners will have to wait for their turn to be brought to King

Yama for the review of their life records and the determination of their sentences.

The sentences meted out by King Yama will invariably send non-believers to one of Di Yu's eighteen levels, where they will be punished according to the specialty of each hell. Because of the sheer number of cases, both the cold and hot hells will be full of the condemned, keeping busy all of King Yama's demonic torturers. Each of the nine groups singled out by the Maitreya, however, will be flung into Abi City, the deepest and most horrible of Di Yu's hot hells.

Going through the book, I gradually noticed that the nine groups represented an eclectic mix of people in the Philippines. I found this odd since this meant that the scope of the sect's beliefs on salvation and punishment was not limited to the Chinese Filipino community. The first five groups consisted of people who have abused their power. Chapter two involved the Maitreya warning politicians against taking advantage of their positions, explicitly singling out those who dispense public funds to build patronage, while chapter three contained an attack on corrupt bureaucrats. The next two chapters then dealt with errant members of the police and media. Following the chapter on the greediness of the wealthy, however, the Maitreya's focus noticeably shifted to groups of people who have committed various sins.

After the expected warning to kidnappers and other criminals, militant activists were chastised for their disruptive behavior and their devotion to false ideologies. In the same manner, the Catholic clergy and other religious groups were also assailed for spreading the false dharma. I barely had time to think about this rigidity, when I was stunned to read that the last ones addressed by the Maitreya were those who have betrayed their family by selfishly leaving them before the end of the kalpa.

I tried to remain as level-headed as possible as I read the chapter. While I noted that there was still nothing that explicitly linked my family to the Righteous Way of the Loyal Children of Heaven Society, I nevertheless felt that my suspicions had been confirmed.

As I may have probably told you, Miriam and I had a difficult time during our first couple of months in Vancouver as we tried to adjust to our new life without the certainty of employment or the approval of our immigration status. Although we had left Manila with the highest of expectations, the weeks of stagnation had dampened our morale and we began to question if our decision to leave had been rashly made. During this time, the frequent calls from the family were definitely encouraging and comforting. As we gradually settled into our new environment, however, the frequency of these calls decreased and eventually stopped altogether. This bothered me, especially when my attempts to call Manila only led to coldly clipped conversations about how busy things were over there and how they would call me back.

These return calls never materialized, and the best thing I could do was to concentrate on going about with our increasingly busy life. I figured that while they were probably dealing with some issues back there, I had no real reason to worry since they would immediately call if there was an emergency. Consequently, I did not hear from them until two years later, when Raul surprised me by calling to say that he was going to be in town for a couple of days.

Raul and I had been really close while growing up. We had been born months apart, and had gone to the same schools until college. This made him my regular companion, especially during the late night drinking binges of our teens and twenties that occasionally ended in one of Manila's numerous strip joints and massage parlors. All this made Raul's phone call a pleasant surprise, and I really looked forward to wax nostalgic with him over a couple of beers.

On his first night in town, Raul met us for dinner at Yangtze, a small Chinese restaurant that we had recommended for its food and nearness to his hotel. Despite his warm handshake and buss on Miriam's cheek, I knew that things were different as soon as we sat down. Right before we ordered, Raul informed us that he had become a vegetarian, and then declined my offer of a beer. At that moment, I knew that this was not the Raul I grew up with, who regularly boasted of having once gone through three pounds of steak, and whose first words to me when he was released by his kidnappers was that he needed a cold brew.

Although there was sense in Raul's cryptic explanation that he had changed his lifestyle before it was too late, it certainly did not help the flow of our conversation. The drunken reunion that I had expected became an awkward question-and-answer session as Raul quizzed us about our life in Canada, thrice asking if we were content and happy, while only giving general answers about the state of affairs in Manila. Looking back, I should have been more suspicious than anything else, especially when Raul told us towards the end of our dinner that he would be going back to Manila the next day since he had already finished what he needed to do. However, I have to admit that Raul's behavior, which I attributed then to the tendency of people to change over time, left me confused and slightly hurt, so much so that Miriam had to tell me as we talked about things on the way home that it would probably be best to focus on our new life, rather than dwell on things that we couldn't understand.

Together with the contents of that chapter and my earlier observations and recollections, these memories were difficult to accept. Everything—from the presence of the temple to Raul's odd behavior in Vancouver, and even the caretaker's assertion that I was never mentioned in his decade of employment, seemed to make sense. I tried to think of other possibilities and explanations that could shake the absurd notion that my family was entrenched in the sect, and had somewhat disowned me for immigrating right before what they thought was the end of the world. I couldn't think of any, save for the nagging questions of why *tai ma* actually encouraged the decision for me to leave, why Raul would go through the trouble of telling me that he was going to Vancouver and why they even bothered to call me about *tai ma*'s death.

As I continued reading, even these apparent discrepancies began to make sense. I realized that *tai ma* wanted to test my loyalty, and when that didn't work out, they actually tried to get me to repent and go back. Even though I didn't know if she had authored the book, I was certain that *tai ma* was aware of its prophecies. However, for whatever reason, I think she only began indoctrinating and mobilizing the other members of the family shortly after I left, probably because Raul's kidnapping and my departure made her sense that the end of the kalpa was drawing near. This explained the gradual change in the phone calls and the eventual construction of the temple. Additionally, I would think that Raul was instructed to go to Vancouver to find out if we were really intent on staying there. What else could have explained his persistent questions, and the surprising quickness of his visit? My undesirable response must have made an impression on them, since they did not call until they informed me about *tai ma*'s death more than a decade later. If the rule on succession was followed, then the leadership of the sect must have been handed down by then to Aunt Raquel, since Grand Uncle Victor was the only one of his generation who was still alive. Aunt Raquel, or whoever inherited the title of Grand Matriarch of the Righteous Way, must have seen *tai ma*'s death as an opportunity to bring me back and convert me. They probably knew that they would not be able to achieve this by excluding me or doing things that would make me suspicious so they tried to give a sense of as much normalcy as possible, treating me throughout the wake and funeral in the cordial manner that can be expected from long-separated relatives with whom nothing much can be discussed. I was sure that they wanted me to find out about things indirectly though, since they didn't really bother to conceal the evidence, and might have even planted the book in a spot where I was sure to find it.

You can probably tell that all these thoughts were as confusing as they were exhausting. While I certainly didn't discount the possibility that the sequence of events did not play out according to the situation I had just described, I was too engrossed to dwell on this. Not that it would've mattered since I was certain that some form of betrayal and deception had gone into play.

As I finished reading the last portion of the chapter, however, it suddenly occurred to me that I had, in a way, also betrayed them by choosing to leave during a very difficult time. Moreover, if they really believed in the teachings of the sect, didn't their attempts to bring me back indicate that they cared enough to try and save me from what they thought was eternal damnation? The sudden impact of these realizations blurred my surroundings, and as I struggled to flip through the remaining pages, I realized that I wasn't even sure if I was hurt, angry or ashamed, or if any of these were even justifiable.

The last few chapters of the book contained an assortment of technical information as charts and diagrams illustrated the secret knowledge of the Righteous Way of the Loyal Children of Heaven Society. A chapter on cultivating the body through martial arts contained numerous drawings that showed different stances and movements. This was followed by a diverse collection of information on healing, which ranged from the massage of several vital points in the body, to a number of spells written on charms that had to be burned and ingested. A list of chants then accompanied a chapter on meditation, which was followed by several vegetarian recipes. Finally, the last chapter dealt with divination and the use of magic, which mainly revolved around the transfer of *chi* among beings.

Although these last few chapters would have normally been of great interest, I could only read them mechanically. I was still distracted by everything, and to see technical descriptions of burned medicinal charms and the transfer of *chi* to inanimate objects only served to loosen my concentration even more. For some strange reason, I knew that I had to revisit that chapter, and was actually quite relieved when I finished reading the book's last few characters.

While it would have been easy enough to pilfer the book, I somehow felt that I had no claim over it. Additionally, in spite of my emotional state, I was aware that quite some time had passed since I arrived, and that I still hadn't started looking for the documents I needed. This compelled me to immediately start copying the chapter into my notebook. Although my translation of the verse sections may not be poetic, I think that I have captured the meaning of what I managed to copy, which I have reproduced below.

## Chapter Ten:
### *Those Who Have Abandoned their Family*
THE ANCIENT BUDDHA Maitreya opened up the Book of Heaven and took a clear look at all the countries under heaven where those who have selfishly abandoned their family reside without shame. Living in secure apartments and houses with gardens and pools, deceiving themselves by being relieved at having escaped the darkness and gunfire amid the loosening of the earth and the storm of flames, they work without remembering the four sources of gratefulness. Drinking wine and eating meat, disloyal to their ancestors, they reject the Righteous Way.

Among them are those unthinking ones who, upon the first sign of trouble, immediately leave with their wife, son and daughter, going far away, disguising their fear and ambition as opportunity. Relying on these, they work hard and are deaf to the call of the village; however, since their deeds are distanced from the good of their elders, brothers, and sisters, none of their cowardly efforts have merit, and only add to their offenses.

Therefore, during the transformative cataclysm, this type of person will be taken back to hell, never to rise again. If, however, you are willing to clear your heart and see that you want to return, then repent and begin to obey the Righteous Way. Become vegetarian, don't do evil deeds and strengthen your mind and body through meditation and exercise. Once you have repented, then all your transgressions will be forgiven.

The Ancient Buddha looked and saw those who have left
Hiding as if heaven and earth are blind to their sins

In the years of the true dharma all cultivated their karma
In the years of the false dharma virtue has all but disappeared

Twelve thousand years ago we practiced the Way as one family
And now you've cast off the energy of your previous lives

Because of blind ambition and cowardice, you've forgotten your home
Your journeys to the east and the west have confused you

Now you are lost and have no memory of your ancestors
You'll regret this later, when the future kalpa arrives

When the land is barren and the world is in turmoil, you'll return to Di Yu

King Yama will be displeased and will judge harshly

Oxhead and Horse Face will throw you nine hundred
thousand *li* into Abi City
Your soul will forever be tossed among the eighty one
thousand sufferings

I urge you to cleanse from your heart the mundane world,
return, repent
Avoid eternity in Abi City and disgrace to your family

Uphold vegetarianism, respect your parents and walk the
Righteous Way
Live according to the true dharma and King Yama will
send you back to Cloud City

The August Buddha, the great turner of the Dharma Wheel,
looked at those who have brought tears to the Eternal
Venerable Mother's eyes. On the third day of the third
month of the *chia-tzu* year, where will...

AS YOU CAN see, I was unable to copy the chapter in its entirety. The first few paragraphs were difficult to transcribe. My hand kept on trembling as I wrote, perhaps because of all the confusion, or maybe because it was hard to write Chinese characters for the first time since high school. By the bottom portion of the third paragraph, though, I was working at a steady pace, and even felt that I could finish the task soon enough.

Just as I was beginning to get comfortable and my confidence was starting to pick up, something happened that was so strange, confusing and terrifying that each moment still continues to vividly haunt me in slow motion. As I was starting to copy the first part of the verse section, I noticed that the characters seemed to be fading away. At first I thought that my eyes were just getting tired from all the reading, or that I had lost track of time so much that night had fallen and I had forgotten to switch on the lights. However, it soon became clear that the characters were really disappearing. Although I was naturally shocked, I quickly recovered to resume copying as fast as I could. I guess my desire to copy that chapter was just greater than anything else at the time.

Despite my frenetic pace, I only managed to get to where my translation ended. By then, all the characters in the book had disappeared. Even the title and the illustration on the cover page were gone. As I flipped through the empty pages of the crumbling volume though, it occurred to me that it was probably good that I wasn't able to complete copying that whole chapter. Otherwise, what I copied might have disappeared as well. I must have contemplated this for quite some time, since I felt exhausted when I finally stood up. I understood that it was useless for me to look for all those documents and that I had to leave the compound immediately. Just like I was certain that I would be spending the rest of my days waiting and that I would religiously, meritlessly whisper the *Wordless True Sutra* during the times when I was sure that I was alone, I knew that I would never be going back. There was nothing else for me in Manila, and my only consolation was the knowledge that I would be going home in a couple of days.

# The Editor

CHARLES TAN's *fiction has appeared in publications such as* The Digest of Philippine Genre Stories, Philippine Speculative Fiction *and the anthology* The Dragon and the Stars *(ed. by Derwin Mak and Eric Choi). He has contributed nonfiction to websites such as* The Shirley Jackson Awards *(http://www.shirleyjacksonawards.org/),* The World SF Blog *(http://worldsf.wordpress.com/), and* SF Signal *(http://www.sfsignal.com). In 2009, he won the* Last Drink Bird Head *Award for International Activism. He is also a 2011 World Fantasy nominee for the Special Award, Non-Professional category. You can visit his blog, Bibliophile Stalker (http://charles-tan.blogspot.com/), the Philippine Speculative Fiction Sampler (http://philippinespeculativefiction.com/), or Best of Philippine Speculative Fiction 2009 (http://bestphilippinesf.com/).*

CPSIA information can be obtained at www.ICGtesting.com
Printed in the USA
BVOW03s1732040614

355402BV00001B/49/P